The After Party

Saundra E. Harris

Saphari Books, Inc., Maryland

Published by Saphari Books, Inc.
P. O. Box 232
Pasadena, MD 21123-0232
Copyright© 2009 by Saundra E. Harris

Cover Design by Keith Saunders www.mariondesign.com.
Book Layout by www.Bookcovers.com.

ISBN 13: 978- 0-974-5486-2-3

1. Women's Fiction   2. African American Fiction 3. Romance 4. Fiction

First Trade Paper Back Printing:
10 9 8 7 6 5 4 3 2 1

Printed in the United States of America

Dedicated to my parents
Samuel H. & Jacqueline Harris
and my brothers & sisters
Carian, Judy, Billy, and Stacey
I love you all...

Acknowledgements

First, giving honor to God from whom all blessings flow. I never realized how determined I was until I started writing "The Party." I worked full-time, attended school full-time, and was still able to write a book. Honestly, I doubted my ability to pull all that off, but as I write this, I am still working, but school is completed- for now. Graduate school is in the plan, but for now I am enjoying my LIFE.

Of course I want to thank my family for being so very loving and supportive throughout my journey. To my immediate and extended family, thanks for your love and support. Tink, Stacey, and Carian, thanks for traveling with me and helping me with book sales. A special thanks to Aunt Linda, because I did not expect you to read "The Party," but not only did you read it, you spread the word to your friends, coworkers, and church family. Everyone has rallied around this gift that God has bestowed on me by selling, recommending, and spreading the word about my debut novel "The Party."

I have to give special thanks to the USDA Bookstore in Washington, DC and their staff for giving me my first bookstore signing. They took a chance on a first time self-published author when no one else would. I have to thank Mike O'Sullivan of Reprint Books in L'Enfant Plaza,

Washington, DC, who offered me my second book signing and continues to sell out of my first novel. To Nalungo Sayyeed of The Sister Circle Radio Show, on WEAA 88.9 FM Morgan State University Radio for having me on her show and supporting me. She has taught me to accept my blessings, to believe in this gift, and to step out on faith. LaDawn Black who had me on her radio show Love Talk with LaDawn Black on WERQ 92.3 FM in Baltimore.

To the Girls Night Out Book Club; Colleen, Myra, Crystal, Deena, Tershia, Keshia, Shelly, Jackie, Detta, and Veda thanks for your love, support, and the fantastic gift that I take on my travels. To The Circle of Women Book Club; Fontella, Iris, Lisa, Kimberly, Melanie, Karen W., Marie, Pam, Tanya, Wendy, Erin, Jeannette, and Karen W., and The Sister Circle Book Club Members; Crystal, Tonya, Jennifer, Cheryl, Murnie, Charlotte, Tara, and Denine, I thank you all for the love and support that you have shown the book and me.

This novel was born of the overwhelming demand from my fans that were upset at the way in which I ended my debut novel, THE PARTY. The numerous questions regarding the outcome of Benét's marriage, Worthy's recovery, Diandra and Kendra's impending nuptials, Kendra's pregnancy, and Shaeyla's new romance must be answered, they said. Besides the favorite characters, I have added Isis Turner, a female player who is going to stir up the bunch when she goes after someone's man...or men.

I invite everyone to visit my website www.saphari-books.com to read about my upcoming events, signings, and readings. While you're there, write me a few lines by signing my guest book and give me your honest opinion of my books.

I hope "The After Party" brings you as much pleasure, anger, passion, and pain as "The Party." Thanks again for your love and continued support.

Saundra E. Harris

Prologue

*W*ow! *Another year has passed and again I find my-self in the same situation as before. Alone. Single. Alone! Here I am, still harboring feelings for Mitch while wanting to explore more with Solomon. What is a girl to do?*

Despite Mitch's arrogance, his need for total control of his environment and all those around him, something inside me still burns to be with him. I have a yearning to listen to his voice, to feel his hands on my body, to smell his essence, and to bask in his vibe. Yet, Solomon gives me a gentle loving. Slow, sure, and sweet. My body is tuned to his. Solomon also brings me to a fever pitch and touches my soul in a way Mitch never could. Therefore, why then am I torn? Why do I allow myself to be in situations that give men total control? What is it about myself that I don't love? That I find wanting?

Hell I could be worse off. I could be like Worthy, who's had one hell of a year, what with JJ beating her to within an inch of her life over her smoking up his drugs. Alternative-ly, Benét, whose marriage is over and who is in complete denial over the fact that she had a good man and messed it up.

But me...I'm just alone, with a successful business, beautiful home, and loving family and friends. Therefore, why am I griping about my single status? I'm griping because it is so hard to find love. I mean real love. A love that is sure, unconditional, uncompromising, steadfast, uplifting, exhilarating, righteous, faithful and true. Unfortunately the reality is that for women over 35, the number of eligible men dwindles significantly. I don't know if they get crazier as they get older or what, but I do know that soon I am going to have to decide about the direction in which my life is going. As much as I long for Mitch, and lust for Solomon, are either of them good for my soul?

I am going to have to be the gatekeeper to my heart and no one else. That's my resolution for this year.

Shaeyla Andrews awoke to the scent of winter in the air. *What a dream that was,* she said to herself. Yawning into a morning stretch, her mind recalled the questions of her future and thoughts of her past from her dream. *How depressing.* She pushed them from her mind. She didn't want to think about *those* questions. Bounding out of bed, she headed into her en suite to shower. As the water caressed her body, she thought about what she would wear to work. Stepping from the shower to her huge walk-in closet, she selected a hunter green pantsuit, a contrasting silk blouse, and matching pumps.

After she dressed, she walked over to the mirror and looked at her reflection. Unconsciously her mind recalled snippets from her dream. It made her question herself. What was wrong with her that she couldn't find love? No, she wasn't a size eight. She wasn't tall and she wasn't light skinned, but she was strong, intelligent, independent and financially secure. She was a beautiful chocolate brown with coal black hair that reached just beyond her shoulders. Her generous hips and thighs led to a shapely backside. *Damn! Enough of asking yourself why. You don't need a man to define who you are and this year you have to make a resolution. You have to be true to yourself and to your feelings about love.*

The buzzer on her coffee pot brought her out of her self-analysis.

"Time to go to work."

The sounds of her neighborhood coming to life met her as she walked out of her door to head for her office.

The New Years Eve party had been fabulous. The guests had a great time. She, Kendra, and Diandra had fun, but it wasn't nearly as much fun without Benét and Worthy. Her girls were dealing with some serious issues. Shaeyla still had a hard time believing that Kenny had left Benét and that Worthy was a crack addict. They had hard roads to travel. She hoped Worthy's stint in rehab would benefit her. The best news of the evening was Diandra's engagement and Kendra's pregnancy.

Why is my life filled with so much drama?

"Because life happens," she asked and answered herself.

Hell, look at her life. She had broken up with Randy, met, fell in love, and gotten her heart crushed by Mitchell, and now was exploring a relationship with Solomon.

Her mind continued its self-discovery throughout the drive to her office. The sun cresting the horizon greeted

Shaeyla as she sat at her desk preparing her schedule for the day. Resolutely, she pushed her reflections from her mind to focus on the year ahead.

PAST DISAPPOINTMENTS

Chapter 1 - The New Year

Shaeyla placed the last of her Christmas decorations into one of three gray storage bins. She loaded them onto her hand-truck, and wheeled them outside. Cold January air seeped through the sleeves of her thin jacket as she raced across the lawn to her shed. Stacking the bins on top of one another, she slid the trolley to the side, and locked the gate.

Her designer timepiece showed her that she had a few hours before her girls arrived. Entering her state-of-the-art kitchen, she crossed over to the pot simmering on the counter. As she lifted the lid the savory scent of her mother's cream-of-crab soup recipe dressed the air. Opening the door to her stainless steel sub zero refrigerator, she retrieved the ingredients for the makings of a shrimp Caesar salad. Under her counter there was the hidden wine cellar where she retrieved her favorite Merlot. *Benét would never let me forget that I didn't have any meat,* she thought, looking at the light menu.

Removing a chicken from her fridge, she cleaned and seasoned it before placing it in her rotisserie oven.

Walking to the console on the wall, she hit a button and the *Best of Maze featuring Frankie Beverly* filled her house. She danced around her kitchen as she stacked the dishwasher, and rechecked the timers on her slow cooker and rotisserie oven before walking upstairs to change. Shaeyla had exactly one hour before her girls descended on her doorstep.

Today they were having a going away party for Worthy to show her that they were all willing to support her through her addiction. It was not going to be easy, and they couldn't let her down. She even had sparkling cider to serve today for Worthy and Kendra.

She smiled and laughed to herself. *Today was going to be so much fun. They could talk and reminisce about the good old days. Especially about the time they first met and how they forged their bond over the years. Their parents told them they wouldn't remain friends, that women rarely did, but they proved them wrong and remained tight for over twenty years. Wow! We are getting old.*

As she applied the final additions to her make up the doorbell rang; crossing to her window she looked down to see the girls' cars parked in her driveway.

Turning from the window, she bounded down the steps to open the door to her friends.

"Girls! Girls!" she yelled, letting them into the foyer.

They had been to her house too many times not to make themselves at home. As they hung up their coats, they wandered into her sunken living room. The watery winter sun peaked through the blinds of her bay window and caressed the twin ottomans that doubled as her coffee table.

Benét headed for the bar and smiled as she saw the pitcher of strawberry daiquiris sitting on the top.

"I knew you wouldn't forget me," she said while pouring her favorite drink into a glass.

Worthy and Kendra took seats on the sofa. From beneath her lashes Kendra looked at Worthy to see if the bar bothered her and its huge array of drinks. She put out a hand and touched her friend.

"What?" Worthy asked.

"Are you going to be okay with this?" she asked pointing to the bar.

She clicked her tongue. "Girl, please! None of you have to change because I can't control myself. Besides, I'll have you to share whatever Shaeyla has for us."

Kendra and Worthy shared something between them that had always been there, and the other women did not bother to interfere. It was fine with them. We all understood one another but with the two of them; it went a little deeper. Further below the surface and more complex. Hearing her say the words and seeing the look on her face eased Kendra's mind.

"You're right. It'll be just us."

Diandra accepted the glass from the tray Benét was holding as she handed out the drinks. Walking over to Kendra and Worthy on the couch, she handed them their drinks.

"Uhhh, Shaeyla has sparkling cider for the two of you," she laughed though the situation was not amusing. Worthy was the main reason they had gathered today.

Shaeyla walked into the room with a trolley covered with goodies. She spied Benét in the corner of the room refilling her glass. The trolley held an assortment of festive appetizers consisting of fresh pineapple, red globe grapes, and port wine cheese. Also placed in the center was a stack of photos turned face down.

"What are these?" Diandra asked.

She was about to spear a pineapple chunk when she saw the photos.

Shaeyla tapped her hand. "No...I have this all planned out."

Diandra rolled her eyes. "Can we have one day where everything isn't planned to the last detail?"

"Sure, we could start with your wedding." Benét said from across the room.

Diandra snickered, "Or your divorce."

The ladies laughed at the snide comments.

"You know, to an outsider we would sound like a group of betties who didn't like one another," Kendra said from her seat on the couch.

"I'd like to propose a toast," Shaeyla said as she stepped into the center of the room. "Come on Benét, move in closer."

"Step away from the bar," Diandra said comically.

Benét laughed. Shaeyla waited until they all gathered around her.

"Okay, I want each of us to raise our glasses and say a few words."

"Okay, I'll start," Benét said. "I want to thank you all for helping me, for being there for my kids and me this past month."

Worthy spoke up next. "I want to tell you that I thought long and hard about the direction my life took this past year. I am determined to be drug free, but I know I cannot do it alone. I need your help, love, and support."

"Well I want to thank you all for helping me with my wedding and for making me *see* Seven for the wonderful man that he is," Diandra preened.

Kendra sniffed back a sob; "I want to thank God for sending Niall in my life and for blessing me with the life I am carrying within me."

They all turned and eyed Shaeyla expectantly.

"I want to thank God for giving me four support-ive, crazy, funny, kind, and outrageously wonderful sis-ters." She smiled at each of them before raising her glass. "Here's to us."

"Here's to past disappointments, fresh starts, and new beginnings," Worthy summed up.

The women fell back in their seats.

"Alright, let's move downstairs."

Shaeyla had asked Benét to help her finish her basement. She thought it would be good if Benét were busy doing something other than dwelling on the mistakes she made in her marriage. The ladies walked down the steps to the room.

At the bottom of the steps, Worthy, Kendra, and Diandra stood in awe at the transformation. The basement Shaeyla had enjoyed decorating with Randy no longer bore any traces of him. Her once drab lower level was now more to her taste. The mustard toned walls gave the room a soft feel. The crown molding remained white, lending a dramatic contrast to the warm tones Benét had chosen. Shaeyla gave her free reign, and she did not let her down. *It put a small dent in my savings, but it was worth every penny.*

"This is fabulous," the women extolled in unison, their heads turning at once to look at Benét.

"You did this, didn't you?" Diandra asked.

"That's why you were so busy these past few weeks?" Kendra queried.

"Yes to both questions," Benét smiled.

"So what do you all think?" she asked as she stepped into the room to place the heavy tray on the bar.

"We think it looks wonderful!" Worthy said as she walked around the room admiring the various accent pieces. She stopped in front of an African fertility statue.

"Isn't this..." her voice trailed off as she turned a questioning eye to Shaeyla.

"Yes it is and no I'm not," she told her while setting the drinks down. Walking behind her bar, she touched a switch and the plasma screen television appeared from the ceiling.

"Aww shit!" Diandra yelled. "Girl! Seven would die for that."

"Hell, I would die for that," the other ladies replied.

"It's off da hook isn't it? I wish that I had done this a long time ago. It was time to get rid of Randy and install Shaeyla."

"I know that's right," Benét said, heading for the bar.

The girls relaxed on the new brown faux suede sectional, each of them careful not to spill anything. Benét plunked down on the floor in front of Diandra, Worthy, and Kendra. Shaeyla retrieved the turned down photos from the tray and sat on the floor beside her.

Shaeyla held the pictures close to her chest.

"When I started cleaning out the basement I ran across these." She turned the photos face up so her friends could see.

"Do you remember this?" It was a picture of the five of them in elementary school.

"Good grief. I had forgotten about these," Benét said as she was immediately thrust back to the day they all met.

She had on a horrible blue and green plaid dress, with white knit socks pulled up to ashy knees. Shaeyla's plaits were going every which way with her signature dour face. Diandra was smiling in a superstar kind of way, while Kendra stood to the side looking at her friends. Worthy was never one who liked taking pictures. She stood in the background with her hand on her hip. Shaking her head, she handed the photo over to Diandra and watched the expressions on each face as the women looked at themselves. That picture was over thirty years old. They were between the ages of seven and eight.

"I cannot believe you found these," Worthy said. "I hate pictures. They immortalize you, and I always seemed to get caught at my worst."

"I never seemed to smile." Shaeyla said.

"On this one you did," Kendra said, holding up the photo that had gotten Shaeyla the beating of her life.

Her mother had painstakingly pressed her hair and given her two Shirley Temple curls on the side and a curly bang. Each year at picture time, the photographers gave them combs, and she loathed not being able to comb her hair like the white kids. Therefore, she proceeded to comb out her bangs on the side and in the front and the result of that made her look like a scarecrow. The fact that her mother had chosen the ugliest dress in her closet did not seem to help. It was green with an Indian Aztec print. *Hideous.*

"What made you comb your hair like that anyway?" Diandra asked.

"Those damn combs they gave us. I thought that I was white and could comb my hair like them. Momma tore my ass up when I came home and my hair looked like that. And you know back then Momma got every picture the five of us took."

"The best proof, I bet you didn't comb your hair out like that the following year," Kendra laughed.

Shaeyla laughed. "You're right. I didn't."

For the next few hours, the women sat around and talked about old times. The conversation continued through dinner as they went through their years in high school, the bad dates and the expectations they had for the prom. They talked of the dreams and hopes they had for their futures.

"Then life happened," Shaeyla threw in.

"Isn't that the truth? I never thought that I would be in the situation I am in now," Benét said sourly.

"I don't see why not. You created the situation. Your ass knew better than to be fucking around. Then to do it with no protection, humph I don't know about Shaeyla and them, but I know your ass messed up. Kenny was a good man, and he loved you," Diandra told her.

"You think I don't know that," Benét scoffed. A slow tear rolled from her eye.

"Yeah, I can see you do. You've been knocking back those daiquiris since you came in. Drinking is not going to make it better, you know."

"I know. It's not easy being alone. I know what you single ladies are going through, and I don't envy your situations at all."

With that said, Benét changed the subject.

"Enough about me, we're here for Worthy. What time are you supposed to check in on Monday?" she asked.

"I have to be there at eight. Kendra said she'd drive me."

"We are all going with you to the center, Worthy. We have to see for ourselves that this facility is the right one for you," Shaeyla told her.

Worthy sat her fork down and leaned back against her seat. She was going to miss having them all together like this. After Monday she would be confined for 90 days to a life regimented by others.

Shaking off the depressing thoughts she said, "I saw my mother and Jared yesterday."

"How was Jared? You told her that all of us would take turns getting him on the weekends while you're away, right?" Kendra asked. She had a soft spot for Jared.

"He is getting so tall. That's going to be my NBA or NFL player. He's going to make momma some dough," Worthy told them.

Leave it up to Worthy to lighten the mood in the room. "Let's get him educated first, then worry about pro sports later," Benét said.

"Okay, y'all want to shoot some pool or play spades?" Shaeyla asked.

"Let's play spades," Diandra said as she helped to clear the table. "We haven't played in a while and I feel like spanking that ass. You up for it Kendra?"

"Am I up for it. I've been wanting to play spades so bad

that I play it constantly at work. Thank God I'm the boss or else my butt would be fired."

Shaeyla sat the cards down, poured herself a drink and sat at the table ready to show Kendra and Diandra that she and Benét were nothing to mess with. "You ready to run a Boston, girl?"

Benét stretched flexing her arms in front of her, "Am I? Let's do this."

After the ladies left, Shaeyla sat in her window thinking about her life up to this point. She felt out of sorts. Oddly enough she believed that her life had been perfect. *At least it had been until last year.* The changes that she went through with Randy were behind her, yet they continued to color her thoughts and ideas about men.

When she looked back on it, she had beliefs about whom the ideal man was, and she'd believed she had found them in Mitchell Steele. He was the type of man she had always envisioned as her man. He was handsome, educated, worldly, and financially secure. Mitchell made her explore her own mind and expected her to reach her full potential. He called it actualizing. *I actualized. I actualized to the point of no return; it seemed like, with him.* She had tried to be his everything when all he wanted was someone to have sex with, no strings attached. He became a fever in her blood. She wanted to be in his life so bad that she did any and everything he wanted.

Ironically, the song playing on her CD player was Minnie Ripperton's *Back Down Memory Lane.* There had been so many warning signals in her relationship with Mitchell. He'd made sex exciting and fun. He made it easy for her to open up and try new things. However, his arrogance throughout their entire relationship escalated daily. His comments about women and how they needed to play their position and know their role confounded her. Yet she remained silent for fear of losing him when she never had him at all.

The night of the charity ball and the introduction of his fiancée, whom she believed to be a ploy, changed everything. However, Solomon told her that Mitch had been engaged before his meeting her. He'd told his friend to tell her, but Mitch was his own man and did as he pleased. *Then, he was pleasing himself with me.* Boy was she a fool.

Shaeyla kept telling herself, never again, but even as she sat thinking of him, she missed him. Missed the excitement he brought into her life, and the sexual freedom that he gave her. She missed their conversations and outings. Hell, she even missed his daughter. *Picture that, and I don't even do kids.*

His partner Solomon had helped her to get over Mitchell somewhat. They started going to movies, baseball and football games. They talked daily and even had several dinners together. Slowly, but surely she did forget her desire to spend time with Mitchell. Since she continued to have business dealings with his company, Jackson-Steele, she was thankful that on the few occasions she had meetings there Mitchell was away. She didn't know if he planned it that way, but she was grateful for not running into him.

Now she had feelings for Solomon and didn't know

if she could trust them. *Am I transferring my feelings for Mitch to Solomon? Am I selling my soul to say I have a man?* The questions nagged at her. It made her really look at herself. What did she want? She had a career doing what she loved. Four of the most supportive best friends a girl could ask for surrounded her, yet there was something still missing in her life. *Intimacy?* That was it. She was missing the intimacy and connection to another human being. *Like what Kenny and Benét used to have. It is the intimacy that Kendra and Diandra share with Niall and Seven. Maybe even what I used to have with Randy in the first stages of our relationship. I thought I had with Mitchell, but believe I'd found with Solomon.* She did like Solomon. *Maybe even love him, but can I trust him enough with my emotions to throw caution to the wind and ride with it?*

Rising from the window seat, she walked slowly up the stairs to her bedroom. As she undressed and showered, her thoughts turned to her week ahead and what she needed to accomplish. *I need to focus on finding the right man. Come on Shaeyla. You have to get it together.* Silently, mired in pity, she chastised herself. *You have to plan these weddings and showers, not to mention the forthcoming meetings for Jackson-Steele.* Just then she decided that she would give Solomon a chance. She would pursue a relationship with him and try not to let the disappointing relationships of the past color a possible future with him.

Still wired from her day and her thoughts, she pulled out her laptop and began working on a few wedding ideas for her girls.

Worthy watched from the window of her fourth floor walkup for Kendra's truck. She had packed all allowable items, carefully following the guidelines from the center. Her torn and tattered suitcase held her sparse belongings. A duffel bag held a pair of boots, her tennis shoes, toiletries, and a journal Shaeyla had given her over the weekend, telling her to write down her thoughts. It would help the healing process. Shaeyla said addiction because she knew that Worthy was also addicted to the man JJ and the lifestyle he led, as well as the drugs. It was going to be up to her to release him from her memory in order to heal. Kendra had told her that she believed Shaeyla was right, because she believed that once you gave yourself to a person, they would always hold on to a part of you. Good, bad, or indifferent, it mattered not. A part of your aura, a part of your essence, a part of your very soul would forever remain with them.

Even now, as she waited to go to drug rehab... boy, she had to get used to saying that one. She was still thinking of JJ and how she should've been mindful of the fact that he knew she had been stealing his stash. Yet he'd said nothing to her because it enabled him to force her to do his bidding.

As she walked downstairs to meet Kendra, she saw that

the rest of her girls where already in the car. She masked her disappointment, because she thought she would have a few minutes alone with Kendra before picking up the other friends. Not that she wasn't close to all her girl-friends, yet she and Kendra shared something special. They understood each other the way Benét and Shaeyla understood each other. They thought alike, yet not alike. It was hard to explain. When she was with Kendra, she felt normal, and with her other girls she felt as if she was lack-ing in something. Shaeyla, Benét, and Diandra had such powerful personalities that it sometimes overshadowed people. Some have described them as obnoxious, but the truth was that they kept it real and spoke their minds.

* * * * *

Worthy stowed her bags into the back of Kendra's SUV, before taking her seat between Shaeyla and Benét. She eyed their bright eyes and too wide smiles, then looked at Diandra's expectant face as she twisted around in her seat and placed a comforting hand on Worthy's leg.

That touch sparked a cord in Worthy. Her eyes welled. It hit her that for ninety days, she was going to be away from her girls. They were closer to her than her own family. These four women meant so much to her. There wasn't a time in her life that she couldn't recall them being there. They were always together, laughing, joking, eating, drinking, partying...sisters. *What have I done*, her mind screamed, *how am I going to get through this?*

Worthy hadn't realized that she had spoken that last sentence out loud.

"We are here for you," Kendra choked from the drivers seat.

Tears racked Worthy's body. Benét snaked her arm around her and squeezed her hand, while Shaeyla clasped her left hand in a reassuring grip. The emotions within the confines of the vehicle were running high. Then suddenly Shaeyla laughed.

"What's so funny?" Benét asked.

Shaeyla had to lighten the mood. She wanted them to see how this was a positive transition for Worthy, not a death knell. "We are in here crying our eyes out like we are never going to see her again. She's not dying y'all, she's just going to get well."

Understanding what her girl meant, Diandra chimed in, "Shaeyla's right. We are only a phone call away, and we'll be here to visit as often as possible."

The friends began drying their eyes. Kendra turned on some music for background and the women talked the remainder of the ride.

Vast parcels of land and dairy farms surrounded the area as the drive took them to the outskirts of Baltimore County.

"Shit! We are in the middle of nowhere," Worthy scoffed. She folded her arms across her chest. "Why did the judge stick me way out here?"

"They sent you out here because this is the best rehabilitation facility in Maryland."

S haeyla Andrews perused the list of venues she had received from Diandra and Kendra for their wedding and reception. She knew her girls well. Well enough to know that they should do their weddings separately, because of their tastes. They both wanted to celebrate their nuptials in the traditional African American style of jumping the broom but that is where the similarities stopped. Diandra wanted to have a disc jockey playing hip-hop and go-go music, with over 200 guests. Kendra and Niall had decided that they wanted a quiet intimate affair with close family and friends to help them celebrate their nuptials. Besides, Kendra was pregnant and wanted to take her walk before she began to show, while Diandra wanted to have a "hellacious jam."

"Still trying to figure out how you're going to give your girls what they want?" Bilal asked as he went into her office.

Shaeyla threw down the papers in disgust, thankful for the interruption from her assistant. "Yes! I think that I am going to have to enlist Benét in helping me to convince them that there needs to be two weddings instead of one. Hell, I don't even know why they decided to have a double wedding; they are polar opposites of each other."

Headset in place, she punched in Benét's code. Benét answered on the third ring, and without saying hello,

Shaeyla just began talking. "Girl, you have to help me with this wedding! They are driving me crazy. Diandra wants ghetto-chic and Kendra wants casual elegance. One wants large, the other wants small, hip-hop, jazz…girl, I am going bananas trying to figure out how I can make this work."

Finally she stopped, "Benét- Benét…?" she yelled out.

"I'm here; I was just waiting for you to shut-up so that I could get a word in edgewise! Damn, girl…don't you say good morning, good afternoon, or even hello! Is that too much of a stretch for you?" Benét chastised.

"Oops, sorry, hey what's up?" Shaeyla apologized, contrite at her rudeness.

"Hello, I'm fine how, are you?"

"Alright, I get your point."

"No you don't because as usual you're only concerned with yourself. You have to stop being so selfish. Now tell me what's going on, and I'll see what I can do."

"It's the weddings! Kendra wants a relaxed, casual elegant affair with jazz music and no more than 100 people. She wants it in the afternoon, serving light fare, champagne, wine, and flavored teas. Diandra wants straight ghetto fabulous, deejay, and a marching band to announce the bride and groom, after six, so you know you have to feed the people. She is bugging over the price per plate, but damn she wants surf and turf, Moet free flowing, and she wants it to be held at the Renaissance Hotel in downtown Baltimore. Now we know that Seven is not strapped for cash, but damn! He bought her that damn engagement ring, *a house*, and the woman is still asking for more!"

"Okay, how about after we go to visit Worthy Saturday, we go back to your office and try to work this out. Okay?"

"Okay."

"Now put the weddings aside for a minute and let's finalize the showers."

"Girl, people are going to be through with us. You know how we feel when we get invitations in the mail. Now we have the nerve to be planning a baby shower, two bridal showers, and a double wedding that could be two if we can't convince them to compromise."

Benét's watch beeped. "Okay, Look I hate cutting this short but I have to run or else I'm going to be late for class."

"Oh, that's right. This is your first day back since winter break, isn't it?" Shaeyla asked. "So how are you going to handle old boy?"

Benét dreaded facing Christian at school, especially since Kenny told her that he had informed him that she had lost their 'bastard love child.' "I don't know. He called twice since Kenny left, but I didn't answer. I don't know what to say to him, or even if I should say anything. Anyway, let me go. Call me later."

"Alright, be careful." Shaeyla told her friend as she pressed the release button on her phone. She would hate being in the position that Benét was in now, because Shaeyla knew that her girl was in love with her husband *and* her lover.

A s Benét replaced the phone, turning to the mantel of her fireplace, she looked at the gallery of photos of her wedding day and her children at various stages of growth. She remembered all those momentous events in her life. *"Girl you know you screwed up"* she told herself shaking her head. Gingerly, she lifted her hand and traced a finger over the frames of those she loved so dearly. Benét constantly wrangled with her conscience; *yes, she had screwed up her life, royally, and for what? A fuck! Damn...Christian had her nose opened and made her feel very much loved.* Wrestling her thoughts away from her continued lust for her former lover and her desire for her husband, she grabbed her book bag and headed to her car. She had been miserable since New Years Eve and Kenny's stunning revelations to her. The sad part is that she did not know how she was going to get him back. *One thing is for sure; you will not get Kenny back by thinking of Christian.*

Kenny! She had called him several times, and he would not return her calls. She even called his office, but he was always unavailable. Benét wasn't stupid. She knew that his secretary had probably been instructed not to put her phone calls through, yet she kept calling. Everyday! Sometimes two and three times a day determined to make him talk to her. She hated that too, because Benét never begged any one to talk to her regardless of whom was at fault or in the wrong. Her motto was 'silence is golden', yet here she was acting like Shaeyla, blowing up his work and cell phone. She did not have his home phone number because he didn't want her to have it and had instructed Kenny Jr. and Zaria not to give it to her.

The kids were adjusting to the transition to a single parent household and to visiting their father throughout the week. He was supposed to get an apartment in the county, but then he changed his mind and rented a place in Fells Point. Kendall now occupied a large three-bedroom home, with chair rails and crown molding, and ebony stained hardwood floors. "The works" as Jr. said. He loved going to his father's house because of the plasma television Kenny had just purchased. A hot wave of jealousy coursed through Benét. She was jealous that her children were privy to Kenny's inner sanctum, and she was not. She was upset at receiving secondhand info on his life. How was she going to work her way back into Kenny's heart and life? In addition, how was she going to handle Christian?

Benét's introspection carried her through the familiar route to Harris State College she found a parking spot, cut the ignition, and exited the car.

She had not realized how much she missed the interaction with her professors and fellow students, and she was excited to be back on campus. She had been trying to keep busy since her separation by rearranging furniture and doing other small things around the house. Benét had even helped Shaeyla to redecorate her basement.

She had not been able to spend as much time with her girls as she would have liked, but they all were embarking on exciting new chapters in their lives. Diandra was spending more time with Seven and Kendra had her hands full with Niall and her pregnancy. Thankfully, Shaeyla was no longer seeing Mitchell Steele. Had the decision been up to Benét, she could have saved her girl the humiliating treatment that he had dished out to her had she just kept it moving. Nevertheless, Shaeyla had to let her feelings become involved *after* he had stipulated that he only wanted sex from her and nothing else. Now she was beginning to spend more time with Solomon.

"Benét, wait up!"

Benét turned to the sound of her classmate Isis Turner making her way from the parking lot. She watched as her dusky brown hair bounced around her shoulders as she trotted towards her. Isis was a big girl, studying art history. The baby blue pantsuit accentuated her too wide hips, but that did not bother Isis. Let her tell it there were brothers lined up around the block trying to holla at her.

"Hey, girl. How was your break?" Isis asked as she neared Benét.

"It was good and allowed me to get a lot accomplished," Benét lied although they were okay with each other, she did not intend to put her business out there. She just did not know Isis like that. She was not Shaeyla, Diandra, Kendra, or Worthy.

"So what's your first class?" Benét asked her as they walked towards the Student Center.

"It's an elective, girl. For the life of me, I cannot remember the name, but I think the instructor is a Zimmerman or Zifferhaught or something like that. One thing I do know is that it isn't a brother."

Benét heard the regret in Isis' voice as she made that last statement. She always looked for a man. One thing Benét did know was that Isis was the type of sister you did not want around your man. You know the type of woman your mother warned you about. That was Isis. Benét had been around her long enough to know that she was not to be trusted around your man.

"Well it sounds like we have the same class. Its American Pop Culture."

"Oh well, do you want to partner up now?"

"Sure, I'm available whenever. My kids are grown and can take care of themselves."

"And your husband?"

"He can take care of himself also." Benét told her.

After purchasing bagels and coffee they made their way to class.

Kendra called Niall as she made her way to her prenatal visit, "Hey sweetie."

"Hey," Niall responded with a smile. "I'm on my way, just running a little late."

It was funny how he could read her mind. "Don't worry, I'm running late myself, so I'll meet you there."

"Everything okay?"

"Yeah, the movers came for the last of my stuff today, and will be delivering half to our storage unit and the other half to your house."

"To *OUR* house." Niall stated. "What's mine is yours...-"

"And what's mine is mine," Kendra piped up cheekily.

"Ha...ha, very funny," laughed Niall for he knew that she was only joking and was not the least bit selfish. "How are you feeling?" he asked.

"A little better, but this morning sickness is the pits. I'll be glad when it's over."

Niall smiled because he knew that unlike his sisters who suffered through morning sickness, Kendra suffered all day long sickness. He was careful of the types of food they ate and even what they drank. Kendra's sickness is the reason he had stopped bringing her flowers because her hormones had all her senses on overdrive.

"Well we'll talk to the doctor when we see her."

"I'm taking the rest of the week off to unpack and all."

"Cool, I'll do the same, if I know you, you wouldn't hesitate to lift and move things you shouldn't."

"Hey it won't be the first time."

"Well it's your last. You have been independent too damn long. You are carrying precious cargo, our precious cargo, and I will not allow you to lift anything unless it's linen and dishes."

"The kitchen and the bedroom huh James?"

"That's right Florida. Kendra, all jokes aside, I love you, and I am going to take care of you and our baby. Neither of you will want for anything, understand?"

Tears welled in her eyes. She had never cried as much as she did now that she was pregnant. "I love you too, and I can't wait to hold our baby in my arms. So yes, I understand and I thank you."

The tears he heard in her voice moved Niall and he patted his breast pocket. Inside his coat laid a yellow velvet box, which held a heart pendant set in platinum. In its center there was a canary one-carat diamond surrounded by baguette diamonds. The locket opened and Niall already had the pictures in his mind of what would go there, one of them on their wedding day and one of their sons or daughters. He had it simply inscribed *Infiniti*. He could not spoil her enough and Lord help him if they had a daughter, because then he would have two he could spoil.

Kendra was pulling into her doctor's complex. "I'm here now. Do you want me to wait in the lobby for you?"

"No go on up, and I'll be there in ten minutes."

"Okay, love you."

Kendra closed her phone and unsnapped her seatbelt. For the past few days, she had been feeling some discomfort in her stomach. She hid the pain from Niall because she did not want to worry him, but each day the pain got worse. She was thankful that Niall was late, because that would give her an opportunity to speak to Dr. Peoples without him. *It's probably nothing. Just bad cramps,* she told herself. *And if it wasn't?* Closing the door, she set the alarm and headed into the building. She hit the elevator button several times as if that made it come faster. Finally, the car arrived; she entered and leaned against the wall. Stopping at the third floor, she entered the doctor's office, and headed to reception. After signing in, she asked if she could speak to Dr. Peoples. The receptionist advised that she was running late. Biting her lip, she looked away. *Damn!* She would have to voice her fears later.

Diandra sat at her dining room table surrounded by books containing samples of wedding invitations, thank-you notes, and party favors. Her house looked like a miniature wedding shop. There were bridal magazines and dress swatches strewn about her living room, on the couch, chaise, and coffee table. She was at a loss because she liked everything that she saw. She had left a message for Shaeyla to call her so that they could try to complete the wedding plans.

Hell, she knew that she was getting on her nerves, but she wanted her day remembered by all as a unique event. She knew that she should not look at it as an event but it would be the biggest day of her life. Diandra had not realized how much she wanted to get married and have a family until now. She had almost let Seven get away because of her love for roughnecks. Admittedly, Seven was not the type of man she normally would have dealt with, but now she understands that every woman should be able to marry her best friend. Every day with him was fun. He made the time that they spent together new and exciting. Seven always came up with different ways of showing her that he loved, cared, cherished, and needed her in his life.

She remembered their conversation from yesterday as

she asked his opinion on the invitations. He had told her to handle that end and that he would be happy with whatever she decided. Not the answer she wanted to hear and the expression on her face showed that. Seeing her upset, he walked over to her and placed a finger on her chin to look into her eyes. The love she saw shining through them made her lip tremble as a wave of emotion engulfed her. His words, "You're my air," broke the dam that held her tears at bay. Shaking her head at the memory of his words, she settled back to her task.

Hours later, she selected her invitations, and now she was torn between two gowns and three bridesmaid dresses. She had to be considerate of Kendra, because by the time she walked down the aisle, she would be showing, so she was leaning toward a dress with an empire waist. Unfortunately, it would not do Benét, Worthy, or Zaria justice.

"Damn, I'm almost tempted to tell Kendra that we should have two weddings." She said aloud as she placed all but the four books with the designs she liked back into the magazine rack.

Kendra and Niall wanted something small and intimate, but she wanted to invite everybody. *Hell, I am getting married.* She thought to herself, *why shouldn't I get what I want? Why do I have to always compromise?* Picking up the cordless phone on her end table, she punched in Kendra's number. Diandra needed to talk and just as a back up, she was going to call Shaeyla and Benét to get their ideas also.

S wiveling around in her chair to stare out the window, Shaeyla vividly recalled several occasions that warned her that Mitch was not the man for her. She thought back to the numerous conversations that she had with Mitchell when they saw each other. They always had the usual conversations about her wanting a more permanent commitment from him while all he ever wanted was to be a friend. From the beginning, he had told her that all he wanted was to have sex and not get too serious. However, Shaeyla being Shaeyla had plowed ahead and ignored her gut feelings. She had also negated the comments Benét gave her at the outset.

She remembered one conversation that still bothered her. He was upset at the opinion she had formed of him, thoroughly pissed because he thought that she thought him trifling and stupid. It all stemmed from a phone call she had given him one evening, and as he picked up the phone; she could hear a rustling noise in the background. To her it sounded as if he was in the bed, which was odd because it was around 9:30 p.m. his voice was sluggish almost breathless. Shaeyla remembered how her heartbeat doubled. His voice lowered and more relaxed than usual saying "Hullo" into the phone. *He sounded –occupied.* Crestfallen at her train of thought she asked, "Are you busy?"

"Hmmm...mmmm...something like that." His voice labored.

"Oh...want me to call you back?"

"Mmmm-hmmm-hmmm- Huh-huh. Why don't you count to a thousand then call me back?"

Stunned by his statement, all she could utter was, "Alright."

What kind of man says that to a woman he is dealing with? Regardless of what kind of relationship they have, common decency should have prevailed, and he should not have answered the phone. Hell, Mitchell acted as if he had no morals or values, almost as if he disrespected women or just plain out disrespected her. Yes, she had thought he was having sex! *And he didn't like the opinion I had of him! What about the opinion he had of me!*

Besides, Mitch worked very hard while they were together to make sure that the opinion she had of him was a negative one. Any compliments she had given him, he would not accept. The number of little thoughtful items she sent him, he seemed to expect. The things that she did to him and for him, all in the name of hoping he too would love her, clouded her judgment. He made her think that all men treated their women callously. That all men wanted sex partners, and nothing more. He was going to understand exactly what she meant when his baby girl grew up into a beautiful woman and met a man like her dad. As a shiver of loathing raced down her spine, she marveled at her tenacity.

Shrugging her shoulders, she deliberately turned her

thoughts to Solomon. He had been away on an extended business trip, and was due to return. Shaeyla could not believe her good luck in meeting a man like Solomon. Now the two of them complemented each other. They finished each other's sentences; enjoyed talking and being with each other, *and* it didn't feel as if he had to force himself to spend time with her. A wistful expression crossed her face as she willed time to past swiftly so that she could be with Solomon.

Friend or no friend Solomon wanted Shaeyla in his life permanently; he just didn't know it yet. Honestly, she liked him more and more. He was exciting, yes, but he also had a generous spirit about him that he showed not just with her but also with everyone in his circle. Trust the circle was small, because Solomon loved strong when he loved and his dislike ran just as deep. So why was she in this self-doubting mode? *"You know you have this cocky arrogance about you, yet you don't have any self-confidence. You have to stop doubting yourself and your abilities Shaeyla, and learn to love the dynamic woman that you are."* These words were burned in her memory. Solomon had said them to her after the debacle with Mitch, and just before he kissed her. What began as a hesitant discovery of her lips and tongue, ended in an explosion of emotion. Just thinking about making love to him made her horny at the oddest times, because she thought about him more than she should. She did not want to push him nor did she want to act nonchalant, and although he had told her he was falling in love with her, he hadn't mentioned anything of love since then. In truth, she was afraid of her emotions and feelings. She had made the same mistake with Mitch that she had with Randall, and had promised herself that she would not make the same mistake with Solomon. She had sold her soul twice to say she had a man, and she didn't want to do it again. *Lord, let me get this one right.*

Solomon wended his way through the terminal, claimed his luggage from the baggage section, and retrieved his car from the daily parking area. He was oblivious to the stares he received from women as they admired the air of confidence in his walk. Mentally, he went over his schedule while at the same time impatient for his day to be done so that he could be with Shaeyla. He also had not advised Mitchell of his relationship with Shaeyla. He did not answer to any one, but he felt it best, as they were business partners as well as friends to apprise him of the situation. Solomon had no intention of hiding or denying the love he felt for Shaeyla. Outside of her girlfriends, she just wasn't convinced that they should go 'public' with their relationship; Shaeyla's argument was she had endured two relationships that failed miserably. She wanted them to take it slow. While, he wanted to run with their feelings and damn the rest of the world.

Shaeyla was also shaken up by the fact that Benét and Kenny, whose love and relationship she envied and admired was shattered. She had told him the reason behind the separation, and he sympathized with Kenny. He knew that she lived in hopes that her girl and her husband would get it together, but to a man adultery *and a pregnancy* were issues he would not be able to forget. If it were him, he would probably forgive that his woman had cheated because people do make mistakes and the flesh is weak. However, a baby he could not forgive.

His thoughts immediately brought to mind pictures of Shaeyla in the heat of passion and the constriction in his loins made him eager to be with her. Suddenly, the image was replaced with a picture of Shaeyla and Mitch, and he became consumed with jealousy that made him immediately rethink his position on infidelity. *He would never forgive nor forget a betrayal from Shaeyla. He wanted to be the last man she was with and the father of her children!* There were so many things that he loved about her. Her smile, the way in which she embraced life and constantly expressed her love to those she loved by the notes and cards she'd send to let you know she thought of you. The way she stroked his chest and massaged his legs just before gripping them tightly as she slowly placed her hot mouth to his manhood. Those thoughts made him determined to tell Mitch of their relationship with or without Shaeyla's blessing.

As he drove from BWI/Thurgood Marshall Airport to his downtown office complex and pulled in beside Mitch's car, he thought *no time like the present.* Exiting his vehicle, he curbed his desire of calling Shaeyla, leaving it until later. Instead, as he made his way to his office, he instructed his secretary to send her a dozen roses.

Striding into Mitch's office, he rapped on the door once to announce his arrival and stepped over the threshold.

"Hey you're back," Mitch said. "How did the meetings go?"

Shaking his partner's hand Solomon explained the intricate details of their latest contract and the outcome. Once he satisfied his business obligation, he stood up and moved over to the window to observe the view of downtown Baltimore's busy streets.

"Something on your mind," Mitch asked. He could see the tense set of Solomon's face and the rigid set of his shoulders.

"In fact, there is. I need to talk to you about Shaeyla Andrews."

Mitch elevated an eyebrow, "What about her?"

"I don't know how to tell you this, so I'm going to just come out with it...we have been seeing each other since the gala. I also have to tell you that I think you're a fool for letting her get away."

"You say that to me as if it's going to be a problem. I mean our relationship, if that is what you want to call it was exactly what it was- sex. Nothing more nothing less, she just couldn't understand that."

"Hell man, how did you expect her to? Brother, you embarked on a campaign to get her with flowers, and dinners, and phone calls; then once you got her, you didn't want her anymore. What was she supposed to think? Your words said one thing and your actions reflected another."

"Look, how I handle my women is none of your concern."

"True, but I made Shaeyla my concern, so just make sure to avoid her in the future."

Spreading his arms wide, Mitch replied, "She's all yours brother."

Eyeing his friend from head to toe, Solomon was amazed at the complacency with which Mitch treated his women. He was the player to end all players, and at one time, he admired that and was even jealous of the fact that Mitch could get women wanting him, lusting for him without trying. However, since his involvement with Shaeyla where he witnessed firsthand how the callous treatment affected her, he pitied the women Mitch dealt with.

"So, how's your fiancée?" Solomon asked.

Mitch placed a hand over his eyes, "Man, I'm thinking of removing myself from this situation. Since the engagement she has become clingy, wanting, and needy, and I won't stand for that."

"Mitch, sometimes you have to learn to take the good with the bad. That's one issue you are going to have to deal with in a relationship. If you felt that way, why did you ask her to marry you?"

"Because she wasn't the clinging, insecure type of woman that Shaeyla is," he shot back. "She was acting like a codependent, being passive and aggressive by trying to manipulate my feelings for her. I told her I didn't want a relationship. So is it my fault that she fell for me and it bit her in the ass?"

At his words, Solomon strode across the room to stand toe-to-toe with Mitch. "First of all, Shaeyla wouldn't have been insecure, had you acted differently, and that will be the last time you speak about her in a derogatory or negative manner. She is a fantastic woman, plus she is still a consultant for this company and will be escorting me to many industry events."

Seeing the irate look on his friend's face, Mitch backed off *for now* he thought. *He knew Shaeyla. Without a doubt, he knew that he was in her blood and with one phone call, he could have her again.* "You deal with it. That is something that I refuse to put up with. I need a secure woman, not someone questioning my actions, words, thoughts, and deeds."

Solomon digested this information before speaking. "Damn Mitch, you have to admit that you enjoyed your women, and took pleasure in them as well as others. I'm sure she knows that. Also, had you even tried to make her feel secure?"

"Man listen, don't come off..."

"No, just hear me out. You make no bones about commenting on how good a woman looks in front of your women. How do you think that makes them feel?"

"That's why I said I need a secure sister. Shit, I like beauty just like you."

"True, but you don't have to constantly comment on it, especially in their presence. I don't care what you say in front of me, but you need to be respectful of the sisters your with."

Mitch turned away from Solomon, telling him without words that their argument was over. *I hate doing it to my man, but once my woman, always my woman.*

S olomon left his friend and strode to his own office. He sat down at his desk and picked up his phone to call Shaeyla. His palms were clammy, and his heart skipped a beat at the thought of hearing her smoky voice over the phone. His mind fast-forwarded to that night, when he could trace her body with his hands and explore her luscious lips and hot mouth with his tongue. Damn, this was the second time today that thoughts of her had him aroused like a schoolboy.

"Events to Remember this is Bilal, how can I help you?"

"Solomon here, is she available?"

"Is she? I'm glad your back, she's been on pins and needles waiting for your return, and the flowers just arrived so your call is on time."

"Is that right? That's good, because I can't wait to talk to her."

"Okay, take care."

"Peace."

"Shaeyla Andrews."

Solomon's heart raced, "Hello beautiful, did you miss me?"

Shaeyla sat back in her chair and smiled, giddy as a teenager. "Yes I missed you and thank you for the roses, they are beautiful."

"My pleasure. So what time are you leaving?"

"Now if you want me."

"If I want you? Woman I've been aching for you since I left. Tonight you're in trouble, because I'm going to tear that ass up!"

"Good I can't wait. I've been longing for you too. I cannot wait to slide my mouth over your juicy...boy I am getting wet just thinking about you. I'm leaving now..."

With that, she replaced the receiver, grabbed her purse and headed to her car to rush home to get ready for her evening.

◆ ◆ ◆ ◆ ◆

Solomon replaced his phone, plucked his coat from the back of his chair, and shrugged into it as he walked past his secretary informing her that he left for the evening and would probably be out the next day.

On his way home, he stopped to pick up her favorite bottle of Italian Merlot along with 12-stemmed strawberries, juicy red globe grapes, and a variety of cheeses to tempt her palette.

Rounding the corner to her home, he noticed that she had left her garage door open. He pulled beside her car, and as he began to retrieve the items from the passenger seat, the door to the garage began to descend. Solomon swung around to find her standing in the doorway in a sheer black bra, thongs, and garter, with sexy thigh high stockings and stilettos. Smiling as he walked towards her with his manhood straining against his zipper, he placed his bags on the floor and backed her into the house. Tethering her hands in his, he placed them above her head. With her back against the wall, he delved into her mouth like a man trying to quench his thirst. Pulling away from her, he trailed his tongue around her lips, and then pulled her head back exposing her dark brown neck. Breathing in the musky scent of her perfume mixed with the dewy essence of her scent drove him crazy. Bending his head, he kissed, stroked, and caressed her making her knees buckle and he had not even touched her breast.

"Damn, I missed you!" she said breathlessly, reaching down to caress him through his pants. She felt his erection and wanted to drop to her knees to take him into her mouth. "Uhhh, p-please" she moaned.

"Please what," he asked as his hands moved to her protruding nipples. He loved her nipples. He loved watching them swell and grow under her arousal.

"Please Solomon do this," he asked as he flicked a thumb over her large orb. "Or is it this you want," he asked as he slid a hand down her body to the heat emanating from her center.

She was hot and ready for him and as much as he wanted to take her there in the kitchen he wanted to prolong the foreplay.

Easing him away from her, "Naw...I want you hotter than you've ever been. I want your complete surrender tonight, Shaeyla, nothing less will do." He wanted no one and nothing on her mind but him.

Moving away from her, he picked up the bags from the floor to place them on the counter. He had not felt this aching need for a woman since Vanessa. *Now where did that come from?*

Shaeyla watched as he tried to regain control of his emotions. A fresh bead of sweat was trickling between her breasts. Gingerly, she walked toward him and placed her arms around his waist. She felt him tense. At her touch, he muttered something unintelligible under his breath, before turning to lift her up placing her on the countertop. Moving between her legs, he pulled the straps of her bra down uncovering her twin cocoa peaks. He traced a trail of kisses from her neck to her luscious full breasts, which fit firmly in his palms. Gently, he kneaded them, before tracing his tongue around an engorged nipple.

Her stomach dropped at the feel of his hot tongue and warm breath as she lovingly gripped his head to her breast allowing him to suckle on her. She threw her head back. Her excitement built in her center when Solomon placed hot open-mouthed kisses from her breast to her belly button. He flicked his tongue around her belly button, making her stomach muscles contract.

He could feel her body jerk as he traced the kisses on her body. His ultimate goal was to reacquaint himself with the taste of her plush center. He needed to immerse himself within her. Reaching his goal the heat that met him as he gripped her body closer to his was intoxicating. He had to be mindful not to cum, as her readiness for *this*, for him had him harder than ever.

He remembered how she liked to be eaten. She'd only had to tell him once. He eased his tongue slowly around the core of her inner lips. He knew that drove her crazy and he was not disappointed as she spread her legs granting him farther access to her. He caressed her with his fingers. Mentally, he talked to her core, coaxing, and goading her clitoris watching it swell beneath his taunts.

"Ahhhh...yeah-h-hhhh..." he heard her moan. Feeling his fingers delve deeper into her "Ahhh...Sol-" his name was cut short from her lips.

Leaning up on his arm, he watched the display of emotions on her face as he moved his fingers within her to her g-spot. He knew that he hit his target when she grabbed his hand forcing him in place. He let her ride his hand, before stilling her. Her cries of protest were soon replaced with sighs of pleasure as his tongue devoured her.

She enjoyed watching him go down on her. She leaned up on her arms to see him as he feasted on her like a starving man who had not had a meal in ages. Lightly, she ran her hands over his head as he looked up into her eyes and the ecstasy he witnessed made him slow down his tongue. He probed with deep long strokes, flicking his tongue over her clit as he made love to her with his mouth.

Her hips rose to meet his strokes while she begged him to stop.

"Please Solomon. Let me taste you."

She loved the feeling of him sliding in and out of her mouth. It made her climax repeatedly.

His negative response created a current of vibrations through her. The action drove his tongue deep within her.

He took his mouth away long enough to tell her, "Cum for me"

"No—"

"I want to taste you," he said before stroking her clit.

"N-No"

Her denial was unacceptable, "Cum for me," he demanded caressing her clit in feather light strokes with his thumb, as his fingers teased her to acquiesce.

Shaeyla could hold out no longer. Waves of ecstasy rippled through her body causing her to convulse with pleasure.

Solomon watched her body stiffen. He lapped up her essence trickling from her middle. *Damn! Her juices were sweet.* After satisfying himself that he had tasted all of her, without wasting a drop, he smacked her butt.

She jumped at his hand connecting with her bottom.

"Boy that hurt," she told him rubbing her hand over her backside.

He leaned down to replace her hand with his mouth. "Sorry, baby. You go freshen up, I'll start dinner."

Shaeyla hopped down from her counter and headed up the back stairs to her bedroom. Since she was partly undressed she removed her stockings and entered the bathroom. She caught sight of herself in the mirror, seeing slight markings from the teasing Solomon had just given her. She smiled, turned on the shower and thought how she was going to *tease* him back.

Isis spotted him when she stepped through the doors of the mathematics building. He stood tall, with his back to her, but all she saw was a light-skinned brother and that was enough for her. Truth be told, Isis loved men. All men, short, fat, skinny, tall, dark skinned, light skinned; it did not matter. All she saw was a man and hoped like hell he was single. Determined to introduce herself, she was disappointed when another equally fine brother took up his attention. This one was tall and brown, with a close-cropped haircut, expensive cut suit, and a smoking pair of black Stacy Adams. *"Damn, two for one!"* she crowed to herself.

She was glad that Benét was not around, as much as she liked her, she knew that both brothers would've gone for her more shapely curves than her own more voluptuous figure.

Don't get it twisted, she thought; she was extra large, but she had always been told that she was a cute girl. Her gray green eyes, she used to her advantage. The braces she had worn as a child had been the bane of her existence during her teen years. The girls had ruthlessly teased her in her neighborhood. As a teenager, she had put that down to the fact that they were not as smart as she was then as her dad had said, "Don't worry baby girl, they are still entrapped in that nigger mentality." If she was honest, she would have been a sight back then, thick brown-rimmed geek glasses, and braces! She had tried to fit in, but never seemed able to make it. Her memories made a shiver run down her spine. With a twist of her long brown curly hair, she made a mental note to linger after class in the hopes of catching one or both in the hallway. As she caught up to the gentlemen, she overheard them talking to one another in clipped tone.

• • • • •

Christian was pissed! The dean had just informed him that in his absence the interim professor had scheduled a lecture for juniors and seniors with Kendall Grier of Jackson-Steele Consulting. He wanted to hit something. No, not something, *someone*. In his anger, he slammed his hand against the wall. Benét's face swam before his eyes, just as a voice said, "Kane."

Turning he found his worst nightmare. Benét's husband Kendall Grier.

"Grier," he spit out.

The two men stood eyeing each other. To an observer it almost looked as if they were in a mental standoff that could become physical given half the chance.

Kendall had spoken to a Thomas Kincaid, who was filling in for Kane during his leave of absence. That is the only reason he agreed to the lecture. Kane was nowhere around. Now he shows up today and comes face to face with his wife's lover.

Kendall was on the verge of saying more, when he became aware of a young woman in a startling baby blue track suit with '*Sof' N Wet*' emblazoned on the front caught his attention. With brown curls that framed her face, she appeared to be standing there listening to their conversation. Her pace quickened as she became conscious of them observing her eavesdropping. As she paused, Kendall returned his attention to the man in front of him.

Clinching his fists, he could feel himself revert to the days he spent in the hood with his cousins.

"I would love nothing better than to clock your mother fucking ass right now" he said with a glare in his eye, "But as a professional, I'm going to do the job that I came to do. Going forward I will send someone else to cover the lecture series for this division." That said, he turned on his heel and opened the doors to head to the podium to begin his lecture.

Isis opened the door to her math class and couldn't wait for it to be over. She could not wait to see Benét so she could tell her about the fine ass brothers she had seen today. She was glad that she had met someone decent enough to be seen with...because she hated hanging out with ugly women. Hell, they only attracted ugly ass men, and although she was heavy, she knew that she was not a bad looking woman. Isis' complexion was golden brown. She wore a 40D bra, and was wider left to right, as opposed to than front to back. She had no ass, and her stomach was not protruding grotesquely, she was a plump size twenty-two, and never had a problem pulling a man.

As the teacher walked in the room she tried in vain to concentrate on the content matter, but math had never been a problem for her. She had always done well in high school, was a member of the national honor society, the student government, and served all four years as class president, so school was a breeze. Isis just needed to get out of the house and do something with herself after her divorce. Especially since she had married and divorced well, and school afforded her a new diversion, and the pick of the litter. She always kept an eye out for the brothers...always! Professor, administrator, student, it did not matter, so long as she got her thing off.

Finally, as she finished her usual pop quiz, she gathered her belongings, and moved into the hallway. She had to find that brother that was in the hallway today. Both were fine, but something about the brown-skinned brother caught her eye. She had found out in class that the light-skinned green-eyed brother was the head of engineering and that he was strictly business. Plenty of the ladies on campus wanted his fine ass, and they could have him because she saw what she wanted.

Peering through the doors along the hall, she was about to give up when she spotted him in the lecture hall. Opening the door she slipped into the first available seat, her eyes and thoughts on one thing and one thing only... the man on stage. *Who was he? Where did he come from? Was he married?* Hell she didn't care if he was married or not. Matrimonial entanglements never stopped her in the past, and it wouldn't stop her now.

Benét packed up her books dreading the thought of having to go to the math building. She had been avoiding Christian since last year, despite the number of times he called. She figured that when he left the hospital that would have been the last time she'd see him. He had left her numerous messages professing his hurt and betrayal, yet he still loved her and wanted to talk to her. She had left them unanswered, hoping he would get the message. Benet knew her affair with Christian was a mistake. But her biggest mistake was she was having unprotected sex that resulted in a pregnancy. A pregnancy she had known nothing about, yet miscarried because of her car accident. When her husband had been told about the baby he immediately knew it wasn't his. Thus her world spun out of control from that point forward.

As she reached the doors to the building, she didn't notice the two men coming from the lecture hall, nor did she see Isis behind them.

• • • • •

Christian and Kenny came to a halt as they exited the lecture hall and their eyes settled on Benét.

Benét's worst nightmare had come to life. She stopped in her tracks, her stance uneasy as she eyed both men warily. The butterflies danced in her stomach. *Should I say hello?* Confusion engulfed her face.

"H-H-Hello Kenny." She did not feel her book bag slip from her sweaty hands to the floor.

"Christian," acknowledging him with a nod of her head as she pressed a hand to her quivering middle.

The hard glares coming from the men were daunting. She had never felt such anger and rage directed towards her. Neither saluted her in greeting; furiously they looked at her, shook their heads and walked on.

In the background, Isis watched as the two men looked at Benét. *Well, looky here,* she thought as she felt the tension in the air. Without any one saying a word, she could tell that somehow Benét was or had been involved with these men.

Benét watched with hooded eyes as they walked away from her. Sensing that she was not alone, she saw Isis standing to the side. *Damn! Had she been there the entire time?*

"Hey girl. I didn't see you standing there."

Isis did not say a word at first. She was still trying to work out the scene that had played before her. She hoped like hell that Benét had not been involved with the brother that gave the lecture. She did not care too much about Professor Kane; he was too much of a pretty boy for her. No, she wanted the brother Benét had called Kenny.

"Yes, I've been here the entire time. So what was that all about?"

"What was what all about?" Benét asked playing for time.

"Sister girl, one thing you are not, is stupid, nor am

I. Those brothers did not have anything to say to you. So what gives?"

Benét was not going to give Isis a hint into her private life, instead, she replied, "I don't know what you're talking about."

So she's playing me for stupid, Isis thought. Benét's belligerent stance warned Isis not to push. *There will be time enough for that later.*

"Okay, Benét. I'll leave it alone for now."

"No Isis, we are going to leave it alone, period,"

Benét scooped her bag from the floor and headed out of the door. She didn't bother to look back, but rolled her eyes in her head silently admitting that she had a narrow escape from Isis' nosy ass. When she got to her car, she pulled out her cell phone to call Shaeyla. She wouldn't believe what had just happened to her.

Diandra froze as she heard the beep of her cell phone. She stilled, not sure if she was dreaming or what. Then, it came again. Beep. The sound notified her that she had received a text message. Rolling to her side her eyes focused on the glow from her alarm clock before scanning the room and focusing on her cell phone. Her eyes widened as she noted the time. *Three o'clock!* Slipping the covers back, she moved gingerly from the bed so as not to wake Seven. Silently, she moved in the darkened space. Her eyes trained on the orange glow from her cell phone. As she picked it up off the dresser, she moved quietly and swiftly to the bathroom. Once inside she looked at the screen to see five messages received. Her stomach dropped as her heart began to beat rapidly in her chest. Without looking at the messages she knew who they were from. *Mason!* What does he want? She wondered. She had stopped going with him the minute she realized her love for Seven. In two months time she was getting married, yet her ego was stoked at the thought of Mason wanting her.

All his messages said the same thing.

"Call me or I will come to see you."

Her hands moving swiftly over the small keypad she typed in, "Leave me alone Mason," and with that she flipped her phone closed and turned it off. He won't be sending her any more messages that night.

Quietly, she opened the door and padded across the room back to the bed. She slid in just as silently as she slid out. With a sigh, she wrapped her arms around Seven's torso and fell back to sleep.

She didn't notice that Seven opened his eyes the moment she left the bed. He watched as she moved to her cell phone and closed herself in the bathroom. He expected to hear voices, but instead he heard nothing. *What are you up to, Diandra?* He didn't want to be suspicious but her phone had beeped at least five times before she awoke. He'd heard the sound immediately, but did not feel he had the right to encroach on her privacy. *Yet she looked scared and guilty* he thought. No, he was not going to trip. In a couple of months she'd be his and she knew that he demanded and respected complete fidelity.

Turning over he wrapped his arms around her and heard her sigh as she settled into a deeper sleep.

The next morning, Diandra woke to sounds of Seven showering. With a wide yawn, she rolled over and stretched before pushing herself up and out of the bed.

She walked to the dresser and picked up her phone. Flipping it on and open, she noticed a new text message and one voice message. She knew it was from Mason. As she scrolled through her messages, she didn't hear the shower turn off. She was so engrossed in what Mason had to say.

"When you least expect me, that's when you'll see me."

Seven saw her face in the mirror.

"Everything okay?" he asked as he towel dried his hair.

She jumped not having heard him enter the room. He always did walk silently.

"Yes, why do you ask?"

"I don't know, maybe because you're chewing on your bottom lip."

"What?"

"Yeah, you do that when you're nervous or upset about something."

She scoffed, "You crazy."

He didn't have time for her word manipulations this morning; he had an assignment.

Diandra was silent as she prepared for work. She was going over what Mason had said. What did it mean? Would he show up when she was alone or with her girls? Diandra didn't know and Mason *knew* that she hated not knowing shit.

Seven kissed her goodbye before he left the house. A couple of minutes later she left also. Her mind clouded with thoughts of two men when it should have been concerned with only one.

Diandra tied the cape in place around her customer's neck. As she picked up the blow dryer to begin drying Ms. Ingles gray tresses, Mason's car pulled up to the curb.

What does he want? She watched him as he exited his car, and made his way to the shop door. Leaning over, she pressed the buzzer to let him in and instructed her assistant to dry Ms. Ingles as she turned and walked into her office.

Mason followed her into her inner sanctum and watched her close the door before sitting down in front of her desk.

She casually asked "So what brings you here?"

Leaning back in his seat, he eyed her up and down. His eyes moved to the bling-bling on her left hand.

"So the word on the street was right?" he said nodding to her finger.

Her eyes followed his stare towards her hand. She lifted her hand up so that he could get a better look at her diamond.

"Yes."

Standing up to make his way around her desk, he grabbed her hand and placed his over the diamond.

"Come on now...you can't seriously want to marry this dude?"

She watched as he stepped closer. Mason aroused old feelings of want and desire within her. Call her crazy, but as much as she loved Seven, Mason was the dick slinger of all time. Seven's loving was the slow kind- *always*. Rarely could she be spontaneous with him, but with Mason, hell, they fucked any and everywhere. He was that type of nigga.

"Mason, why did you come here? We haven't spoken or seen each other for months. Then suddenly, you start sending me messages and leaving me voice-mails because you heard that I was getting married."

"Come on, Shorty," he said, while pulling her closer to him.

She shrugged his hands off her and wrenched herself out of his embrace.

"No! Mason. It ain't even that type of party. Regardless of what you may think, I love Seven, he's a good man and I'm not going to mess my relationship up fooling with your trifling ass." She walked over to the door and pulled it open.

He stood staring at her before leisurely walking to-wards the door and taking it from her hands, closed it to the nosy eyes outside it. "Is that right? I know dat nigga ain't giving you the dick like I did. 'Member how it used to be with us, Dia? How you used to scream my name, and beg me to nibble your back?"

Backing away from him, his words brought to life im-ages of the two of them together. Images of how they used to be. She couldn't look him in his face for he would see the truth there. Yes, she remembered how they used to be...he gave her the best fucks of her life. She felt her nipples tighten at the picture in her mind. The two of them tangled amongst the sheets drenched in sweat from their vigorous fucking. *Come on Dia get a grip!* Her conscious screamed. Mason only fucked her, while Seven made love to her. Cherished and adored her.

Mason watched the desire enter her face and saw her nipples begin to protrude through her thin T-shirt.

"I see that you do remember."

The smug look on his face brought her back to reality.

"So what! I remember! That still doesn't mean anything."

She watched his nostrils flare and his lips grow thin, showing his anger at having his plans backfire.

"Prove it then. Go out with me next weekend."

Diandra couldn't believe him. "Shit, for real though, bruh it's time for you to bounce. Go holla at one of your hoochies if your dick is hard."

Stopping at the door, she turned as she pointed to the vee between her legs 'Cause dis pussy here, you will never taste again…it belongs to Seven now." With that as her parting shot, she opened the door and returned to her customers.

The chatter in the shop stilled as she headed to her station. All eyes were on Mason as he trailed behind her. Picking up the curlers, she watched him stroll past her.

When he reached the door, he turned smiling, "Imma holla at chu lata."

Turning her back to him, she directed her attention to her client.

Seven rounded the corner and stopped. He immediately recognized Mason's cherry red Hummer parked a few feet from Diandra's shop. Anger engulfed him as he raced across the street. He was only but a few feet away when the Hummer roared away from the curb. Slapping his side in frustration, he turned back toward Diandra's shop. He needed to know just what was going on.

Diandra looked up in surprise as she saw Seven leaning on the buzzer. No sooner had she pressed the release catch than he pulled the door open roughly and stomped towards her. Looking at her client earnestly, he excused himself and dragged her behind him to her office.

Diandra was embarrassed and humiliated as she spied the eyes of her clients and co-workers looking at them in disbelief. She knew that half of Baltimore would know about this scene before she got out of the room. Hell, Mason had just left so she knew that rumors would abound.

He jerked her to the office and slammed her into the chair. He swiveled her around to face him. Right now, all he wanted to do was slap the piss out of her mouth. However, he was never one for laying hands on a woman.

"What the fuck is wrong with you?" she asked shakily.

She had never seen Seven in this type of mood. He looked as if he could hit her.

"Cut the bullshit Diandra! I saw Mason's ride outside and I want to know why he was here?"

Deny, deny, deny the lie, she repeated to herself. *Think D, think! Tell the truth or tell a lie?*

"What! Is that what the fuck this is about?" she asked.

As she tried to push past him and stand up, he held her in place with his forefinger and a look.

Reclining in her seat, she stated forcefully, "For your information, Mason dropped off one of his girls. Lisa does her hair. Are you satisfied now?"

The lie slipped from her lips easily. She stared him down daring him to question her.

Seven looked her square in the eye. "Is that right? So you won't mind my asking Lisa about that now, would you?" he said as he turned and headed back to the salon area.

Diandra jumped. She had to make him believe her and trust in her and what better way to do that than to question him.

"Go ahead and ask her. But if you don't trust me enough to believe in me and have faith in me then I don't see how I can even contemplate marrying you."

She never realized the truth of this statement until she said the words. Yes, she loved Seven, and she knew that having Mason in the shop was wrong, but she was damned if he was going to go Neanderthal on her and embarrass her.

"And another thing. You need to apologize to me for humiliating me on my job, but you also need to apologize to my employees and customers. You placed them in the middle of something that should have remained private."

With that stated, she swiveled around to return to her customer when he stopped her.

Her words made him feel small. He had embarrassed her at work. He had placed people in the middle of their private life. However, when she asked why she should marry him, he began to have doubts. One thing for sure is that he knew he couldn't live without her.

All he could think to say was, "I'm sorry."

"Yes, you are sorry."

"I know, but I saw Mason's ride and went ballistic. I love you."

"Well you have a damn sure funny way of showing it."

"I love you, Diandra. No don't turn your head away from me, I love you and I'm sorry for coming in here like a jackass."

When she still didn't respond, he pulled her into his arms.

In his arms was where she wanted to be, but she decided to make him sweat some more. She kept her body rigid not lifting her arms to embrace him.

"What can I do to make it right?" he asked.

"Trust that I love you. That the type of man that Mason is and what he represents doesn't interest me anymore. Until you realize that, I think we may need to rethink our commitment to each other."

"No we don't need to rethink our commitment, because I know that I love you."

Diandra stood silently as he talked, then watched as his eyes pierced hers. "But understand that this is the last time I want to come here and see your ex."

She sucked her teeth. "I said his girl gets her hair done here."

"I don't care. Either get rid of the stylist or the client, it matters not to me. But I don't want to see Mason Daniels in this shop again."

"You can't tell me how to run my shop."

"If you say there is nothing going on between the two of you, then this won't be an issue."

Having said that, he placed a kiss on her forehead and started towards the door. With his hand on the knob, he turned back to view her confused expression.

"Handle it." He said as he walked out the door, through the shop and out of sight.

Shaeyla wouldn't have believed it if she hadn't seen it with her own eyes. Standing near his car locked in a heated discussion stood Solomon and a woman. He had her upper arm gripped in his hand as he talked; his other hand cutting the air incisively emphasizing each word he spoke. The woman in question stood a little over five feet, and looked to be around 130 pounds. Her sandy red waves framed her caramel face, and she was shaking her head in denial to what Solomon was saying.

Who is that woman? She asked herself, and w*hy was he holding her like that?*

The knife of jealousy surged through her being. She tooted her horn to make her presence known and watched as Solomon dropped the woman's arm. He looked annoyed and guilty at the same time, annoyed at the intrusion and guilty at being caught. The woman turned as she too had witnessed the display of emotions crossing Solomon's face and wondered about the cause.

As she parked her car, she didn't move. She didn't know what she should do, if anything. Slowly, she gathered her belongings as all the while questions swam in her head as to the woman in his presence. *Who was she? What was she to him? Why or what are they arguing about?* Her conscience told her to let him explain, but her gut instinctively told her to cut her losses. She could not and would not endure another triangle situation. She endured sharing Randy, and tolerated Mitchell, but Solomon could forget it. She was worthy of a man of her own. Myriad doubts swirled in her mind. Caught up in her reverie she didn't see him approach the car.

Leaning down to her low-slung two-seater, he wrapped on the window. Startled back to the present she slowly turned to him. Shaeyla's face had always been expressive and today was no different. Disappoint, anger, and jealously played across her face.

Solomon knew he had to explain about his ex-girlfriend Vanessa.

As she opened the door to stand before him, the lump that had formed in her throat had settled in her stomach. She didn't have to say anything because her look said it all.

"Shaeyla let me explain. It's not what you think."

Still she said nothing.

A bead of sweat formed on his brow, and as he wiped it away, he pressed the bridge of his nose, not knowing where to begin.

She watched him, knowing that her silence made him nervous. She couldn't believe that this shit was happening again, but with a different caliber of man. She had never bought into the belief that all men cheat or that all men are dogs, but now she wasn't so sure.

Though she looked at him, no words came out of her mouth. Her expression, one of disdain, and she shrugged her shoulders and sat there...waiting.

Solomon stood, perplexed where to begin about him and Vanessa. For all the times for him to get a blast from the past it would be now. They hadn't spoken in a year, yet the sight of her always did something to him. Vanessa had been his salvation at one point in his life.

Tapping her feet, Shaeyla stood there on the pavement waiting for him to begin. "So are you going to talk or what? I don't have all day?"

Solomon was never one to mince words. He believed that honesty was the best policy, but today he felt real fear for the first time because he knew Shaeyla's history and general distrust of men. He knew that he would have to fast-talk her into his story.

Spreading his hands in supplication, he told her the facts and only the facts.

"Like I said, it's not what it looks like. That was Vanessa, my ex fiancée."

Taken aback by his admission, Shaeyla only stared with her mouth open. For the past several months, she thought they'd shared everything, but obviously not.

"Fi...Fi...Fiancée?" Her senses were barely able to form the word.

Solomon reached out as he saw her stumble back. She wrenched away from his touch.

"You're no better than Randy. Hell, you hated the way Mitch treated me and here you go and do the same thing!"

"Shaeyla, listen. We broke off long ago."

"Well it sure as hell didn't look that way to me." She

snorted, "You had her all gripped up, your hand slicing through the air. That's the sign of an angry man!"

Before he had, a chance to think the words burst from his mouth, "No! Yes!"

"Hell, Shaeyla! No, I am not mad, but I am disappointed in the way in which our relationship ended." His baldpate glistened in the sinking twilight. He swiped his sweat-slicked scalp.

Shaeyla wiped her hand over her right eye as if she were trying to see through his muddled explanation. All she could think of was that she was in the same situation *again*.

"Well then Solomon, I suggest you do what it is you need to-to-figure it out, come to grips with your disappointment, your confusion or whatever. One thing that I do know for sure is that it can be best handled alone."

"Alone?"

"Yes. Alone. I am not going to be second best. I am not subjecting myself to another love triangle. I am not waiting around for you to figure this out."

With that as her parting shot, she got into her car and drove off and Solomon turned to finish his conversation with Vanessa.

Shaeyla's foot on the accelerator did not lessen until she rounded the corner to her home. In her distressed state, she did not notice the mint green Jaguar parked on the corner. Tapping the button above her sun visor the monogrammed doors to her garage lifted, closing slowly behind her. Sitting with her head resting on the steering wheel, the memories seared in her mind that she and Solomon had created within her home.

"You are the worst judge of character, Shaeyla Andrews!"

Entering her home, she threw her keys in the tray near the door and dropped her briefcase at her feet. Crossing over to her wine cooler she grabbed the first bottle her hands settled on. She popped the Champagne cork and poured herself a large glass of Chablis, chugging it down like a cheap swill rather than savoring its poignant flavor.

The knock at her door startled her. *Solomon had followed her.* Her palms began to sweat. *What was she going to say to him?* Setting the glass down, she crossed her kitchen and moved into her living room. After taking a deep breath to gear up her courage, she opened the door.

"Solomon, I've said all I have to say-" Her voice trailed off, it wasn't Solomon at her door. It was Mitchell Steele.

His amazing stature engulfed her doorway. The stance

emphasized the force of his thighs. Without asking for an invitation, he walked into her home. Automatically, she moved back. Her anger dissipated in her confusion.

"What are you doing here?" she asked him in astonishment.

His accusing gaze riveted her.

"Now is that anyway to treat your lover?" he asked as he closed the door behind him. "So you were expecting Sol?"

Ignoring his question, she countered with her own.

"Answer the question. What are you doing here?"

Taking his time in answering her, his eyes traveled over her body. He began with her coal black mane pausing to admire her exposed cleavage before continuing his journey downward. He stopped at her middle and moistened his lips before bringing his gaze back to hers. Slowly and deliberately he moved forward, his gaze intent on her. He raised his hand to her face turning it from left to right.

"You've been crying," He stated it as a fact.

She couldn't deny it as she wiped her hand over her face. Brushing him off, she turned and walked into her living room taking a seat on the settee. Crossing her legs Indian style, she hugged her black Tibetan lamb pillow to her chest. Shaeyla was weary and not up to the oral sparring she knew Mitch was ready to deliver.

He saw her shoulders droop in defeat. Her question resounded in his mind. *What was he doing there?* Initially, it was to drive home his point to Jackson on how vulnerable Shaeyla was. However, seeing her in this state angered him. Sliding down beside her, he placed an arm around her and felt her stiffen under his touch.

His touch opened the floodgate of tears that she had been holding back. Of all people to see her in this state, it had to be him.

Solomon returned home dejected and frustrated. The questions in his mind were endless. *Why had Vanessa returned? Why did Shaeyla have to see the two of them together?* He hadn't really had a chance to explain about his tumultuous relationship with Vanessa to Shaeyla.

He felt it best to leave the past in the past because the past could do nothing but hold you back. He practiced forward movement, yet it was *Vanessa*. Despite his growing feelings for Shaeyla, something inside him still responded to Vanessa. She was the first true love of his life. There was a time when he believed her to be his last.

Slowly, he moved into his den, poured himself a drink and sat down behind his desk. His head lifted swiftly at the sound of Max' paws tapping down the hallway. The large canine placed his head in his lap, as if he instinctively knew he needed the comfort.

"Well ole boy, your master has messed up big time."

The dog lifted his head as if he understood, causing Solomon to gently rub his head as he sipped on his drink.

The glaring sound of the phone interrupted his melancholy moment.

"I'm not answering that," he said aloud; *let the machine get it.*

No sooner had the words left his lips. He heard, "Solomon pick up if you're there."

Vanessa. His eyes were riveted to the machine waiting to hear something profound. After a moment of silence Vanessa continued, "I guess you're not there. Anyway, give me a call when you get this message. My cell number is the same. I am staying at the Hyatt, room 1217, and will be in town for another week." With that last statement, the phone disconnected.

Damn! Who should he talk to first? Vanessa or Shaeyla? Confusion sat on his shoulders. The burden weighed down his body, occupied his mind, and maligned his spirit, yet he had no choice. His first loyalty was to Vanessa. He owed it to himself to hear her out.

Solomon pondered what to do for hours. In the end, he chose to call Vanessa because he couldn't talk to Shaeyla until he did.

• • • • •

The lobby of the Court Hotel was bustling with activity. Solomon pulled out his cell and called Vanessa to tell her he was there.

He moved to sit in one of the comfortable lounge chairs to take in the scene. From the corner of his eye, he saw a movement in white. He turned to see Vanessa descending the escalator. If it was possible, she was even more beautiful now than she was before. The white linen dress tied at the side exposing a teasing shot of her long caramel leg. Her hair was pulled back into a bun, giving her that air of professionalism she had always favored. As she made her way to him, he stood up to gather her in a warm embrace.

"Thanks for seeing me."

"I couldn't not see you," he found himself saying.

For it was true. Something in him was compelled to see her to get the answers to his unasked questions.

"Do you want to stay here and eat in the restaurant upstairs? I heard the view of the city is breathtaking."

Not wanting the temptation of being with her and drinking in a hotel knowing that her bed was only an elevator ride away; he opted to leave the premises.

"How about we go across to the harbor to the seafood restaurant?"

Making their way through the bustling crowd, they made small talk, asking about each other's health and careers. It was unspoken that they would leave their past relationship alone until seated at their table.

Solomon made his way through the throng of patrons. Being there several times over the past year, Solomon was seated by the maitre d immediately.

Once seated with their drinks ordered, they sat in tense silence.

"So I guess you're wondering why I looked you up?"

"The question had entered my mind."

"To be honest, I had to see you again. To see if I still felt the same."

"The same?"

"To see if I was still in love with you."

"Vanessa, let's not go there. You chose your career and I accepted that."

"I know. However... Solomon, please understand that it was what I had to do. I was miserable out west without you, but I had to go. I regretted my decision the minute I said it, but my pride wouldn't let me show it."

Solomon held up his hand. He didn't want her to continue. "Vanessa. Stop. You can't come back here and expect me to take up with you where I left off. You hurt me deeply and it took me a while to get over you."

"I know and I am so sorry for that."

He sighed heavily. "I am seeing someone."

"You mean that woman who saw us today?"

"Yes."

"Well tell her about us and I'm sure she will understand."

"Us? There *is* no us. Haven't you heard a word I said? I am involved now. You had your chance and you blew it."

He could tell by the way she sat back and eyed him that she wasn't going to give up without a fight.

"Okay. Let's not ruin dinner. We are just two friends having a meal for old time's sake."

Not trusting her, Solomon agreed and just hoped he didn't live to regret his decision.

Worthy stood in the mirror eyeing the minor changes to her body. Running her hands over her middle, she looked at the slight pouch of her stomach. *Oh hell naw! I have to lose weight.* She was shocked because she had always maintained a healthy size eight, but her crack diet had taken her body down to a gaunt size four. *What must her girls have thought about her appearance before?*

Lifting her hand, she touched her newly styled mane, wondering at the feel of her soft curls. The sunlight streaming through the windows attested to its healthiness as the rays bounced off Worthy's coffee locks. Her face was fuller lending a softer look to her strong features. Her soft alluring mouth was slightly parted as she stared back at herself. She couldn't believe that it was her own image staring back at her.

I don't look like a crack head anymore! She told herself in amazement. She wondered what her girls would think now. They had been so good to her, sending her clothes and pictures of themselves with their families.

Her mother had sent her pictures of Jared.

Jared! She had failed not only herself, but she had failed her son. *What was she going to tell him? How would he react to seeing her? Her mother? Her girls?*

Her hands trembled at the thought of seeing her girls

again. Today was the first day that she was allowed visitors since she'd arrived at the rehabilitation facility on Chase Street. She was embarrassed at having to be there, yet proud that so far she had been able to stem from her cravings. The counselors told her that she had achieved so much, but they constantly reminded her of the changes she would have to make within herself. She would have to be sure to stay away from men like JJ. She had to take one day at a time. For the last few weeks, her ritual since arriving in rehab had been to accept and admit her addiction. Then she had to learn the serenity prayer and attend her meetings.

The meetings are what she hated the most. Even when she arrived, she thought the other people there were beneath her. She thought that she had her problem under control. The beatings and her lies were part of the lifestyle she led. She thought that she had everyone fooled. Even when her girls tried to do their version of an intervention it didn't stop her. They left her alone for less than five minutes and that's all it took for her to grab her purse and run out the door, down the steps and around the corner to catch the bus home. There she found JJ's stash. On her last hit, he caught her and beat her so badly that she ended up in the hospital. That's when her girls told her she had to go into rehab.

Hell, she got off lucky. She could be sitting in a jail cell. Instead, her girls had talked to her about confessing to the police. Worthy told them everything she knew about JJ and his connections. She knew it was dangerous; knew that if he found her, he would whip her ass again or worse, kill her. But she had to do it.

Turning away from the mirror, she walked from the room to await her girls in the visiting area.

• • • • •

The ladies sat pensively in the visitor's area of the center. They had stopped to see Worthy on their way to Diandra's bachelorette party.

There were posters all over displaying the serenity prayer and the 12 steps. There was also a roster list of visiting dates and hours posted on the wall near the door. Shaeyla, Benét, Diandra, and Kendra were huddled together looking chic as always. Shaeyla was the epitome of sophistication from the top of her midnight-mane styled in layers to the bottoms of her black slides. Diandra sported a designer black and pink velour tracksuit with matching tennis, with Kendra in cute pale green maternity top and chinos and matching flats. Benét wore red from the sporty red cap on her head to the soles of her feet. The men in the center openly stared at her breasts that were on full display in the revealing blouse and skintight pants. One by one, they eyed the black beauties sitting there, wondering who they were visiting.

Worthy rounded the corner and let out a shriek at seeing her friends. The last time she saw them was when they had dropped her off. Since then, there had been no phone calls or anything until today. She smiled as her girls got up to come towards her.

"I'm so glad to see you all," Worthy shrieked as she threw her arms around them.

Their laughter and tears caused the other visitors to

stop and look, some with envy and others with disgust. Releasing her friends, shedding tears as they did the same. Immediately, her friends started talking at once.

"You look great," cried Shaeyla.

Kendra asked, "Are they treating you right?"

"You've picked up weight," Benét chimed.

Jokingly Diandra said, "Even your hair is done."

"Hold up. One at a time," Worthy laughed. She had forgotten how overwhelming her girls could be.

"Yes, I've picked up weight. I needed it and it makes me look good. I've been taking more time with my appearance lately. So yes, my hair is done. As for treating me right, its okay, but it's not home."

"Are you in a room alone?"

"No, unfortunately. I have this roommate named - get this y'all - *Bliss*. Ain't that a bitch? What in the hell was her mother thinking I have no idea."

Shaeyla raised a brow at this because Worthy was not the neatest of people. "How is she as a roommate? Is she clean?"

"Alright I guess. But there is something shady about her. I get the feeling that I've seen her somewhere before, but I can't figure out when or where. Maybe she just has one of those familiar faces, " Worthy shrugged. "I can tell you that she always pushes the rules. The rules are strict too. If your roommate breaks the rules both of you get in trouble."

Diandra furled her brow. "What? Rules?"

"Yes, rules. That you have to follow strictly or else

your visiting rights can be denied, you get extra chores, a bunch of bull shit."

"Then why did you choose this place?" Kendra asked. "It sounds more like prison than rehab."

"I chose it because it's secure. Let's face it. JJ could already be out in the streets. I can't have him finding me--"

Her fear of JJ caused a ripple of trepidation throughout the group.

"Chile, please. Last I heard he was still locked up. So stop worrying," Benét told her.

She had just as much interest in him being locked away as Worthy did. He had hurt her that night also.

"Okay, enough about that loser. We have a lot to catch up on," Kendra said.

The ladies moved to a corner table, somewhat secluded from the rest of the visitors and slowly caught up with the events of each other's life.

Benét went first, bringing Worthy up to speed on her relationship with Kenny. Then Shaeyla went, talking mostly of her business, leaving out the part about Solomon, while Diandra talked of her wedding, and Kendra spoke about the baby.

Before they knew it the time had flown. Visiting time was over and the women had to take their leave. They hugged one another, reluctant to go, for it had been so long since they were all together laughing and cutting up. Worthy walked them to the door and waved until Diandra's truck disappeared from view.

• • • • •

Bliss watched the scene in disgust from her view near the soda machine, hatred for Worthy showing in every pore of her being. Having to be nice was beginning to strain her. For the past month, she tried to get her to confide in her, but Worthy always held back. She never once mentioned JJ. But whether she mentioned him or not was irrelevant. Her mission was to string her out again. To do that, she had to gain her confidence because in three months she would be released and the plan was to befriend her enough so that they could share a place. That's when she could really put her plan into action.

As the girls left Worthy, Diandra noticed they were headed downtown. "Where are we going?" she asked.

Shaeyla turned from her position in the passenger seat. "I thought we'd go downtown and grab a bite to eat. I figured that we could check out that restaurant in the Hyatt."

"I don't have Hyatt money on me," Diandra said.

"Then it'll be my treat. Think of this meal as an early wedding present," Shaeyla said to her and winked at Benét, who was driving.

"Now you're talking. But I wish you'd said something. I could've worn something better than this jogging outfit."

"Girl," Benét piped in, "you look fine."

In the back seat, Kendra sent a text message to Stacey, a girl that worked in Diandra's shop, letting them know that they were on their way.

The ladies chatted about everything and nothing as they drove through downtown Baltimore. Pulling into the valet area of the Hyatt Regency hotel, they exited the SUV and crossed the foyer to the signature glass elevators that overlooked the hotel atrium and the Inner Harbor. They stopped on the ninth floor and the ladies exited the lift.

"I thought y'all said we were going to the restaurant?" Diandra stated.

"We are," Shaeyla said quickly. She hoped not too quickly. "We just have to make a quick stop."

"For what?" Diandra asked.

"Damn, you're nosy." Shaeyla said, "I said I have something to do. And that's that."

Diandra shut her mouth and followed her friends down the corridor to room 920.

Shaeyla knocked and entered the room, with the ladies trailing behind them. Diandra walked in last and as she entered the room completely, the women yelled, "Surprise!"

Diandra was shocked.

"Girlfriend, you didn't expect this did you?" Stacey asked as she stepped to her and gave her a hug. "Congratulations."

Diandra walked around the room giving hugs to her family and friends.

After that she turned to the ladies and said, "Well y'all, lets get this party started!"

Benét knocked on the connecting door before entering. She had been instructed by Shaeyla to call up one or two DC Bad Boys for a night of hedonistic fun for the ladies. Entry was granted by invitation only, because not all women understand the rule. "What goes on at the party stays at the party." That was a standard tried and true rule that had gotten plenty of women uninvited in the past.

Benét danced over to her. "Girl, you have outdone yourself this time," she said as she eyed the Mandingo warrior in the middle of the floor.

Their eyes followed his 230 pound body draped oh so lovely on his six foot three-inch frame. The pseudo manacles he had around his neck, wrists, and ankles made him look like a true Mandingo. The ladies all screamed as he stripped down to nothing.

Fanning her body and reaching into her purse, Shaeyla retrieved a twenty-dollar bill and placed it between her breasts.

The party was jumping and Shaeyla danced around the room singing.

"Party over here!" she whooped out gyrating to the music of P-Funks 'One Nation Under a Groove.' *Hell, this is what she was about, partying and having a good time.*

As the partiers thinned out, Shaeyla and the ladies began to clean the room.

"Look, y'all have done enough. Take Kendra home, she looks wiped out. She needs her rest for her and the little one. I can finish up here," Diandra told them.

Shaeyla looked around. "If you're sure? I cleaned up most of the mess. But you're right, we do need to get Kendra home."

"I can get Seven to come and pick me up. Y'all go 'head and roll out."

Her friends gathered their purses; then the 4 ladies gave their friend one last hug.

"We'll talk tomorrow," Diandra told them.

As they left, Diandra turned to survey the after affects of the party. There wasn't much for her to do and she would be out of there within the hour.

Mason stood in the shadows near the elevator bank. He watched as Diandra's friends got on the lift and descended to the lobby. He observed Shaeyla step to the counter to pay for the room. He heard her state the room number and then watched the three ladies exit the building. He stepped over to the elevator winch and pressed number nine. He was going to see Diandra.

As the pulley carried him to his destination, Stacey from Diandra's shop was returning to the hotel. She had left her cell phone in the room. She had contacted Diandra to let her know she was on her way back to pick it up.

The carriage stopped, and Mason exited. He knocked on Diandra's door.

Diandra opened the door to Stacey with her cell phone in hand. "I know it feels-", the words stopped. It wasn't Stacey at the door but Mason.

As the doors to the elevator opened, Stacey saw Mason entering Diandra's room. She didn't know whether to turn and leave or what to do. She had called Diandra to tell her she was coming to get her phone. Moving down the hall, she stopped in front of the room and could hear muffled voices. She knocked.

Diandra turned to Mason and put her finger to her mouth. She didn't want any one to know he was there.

"Who is it?" she called out.

"It's me," Stacey said.

Diandra opened the door and handed her the cell. Stacey noticed how she blocked the entrance to the room but didn't say a thing. She couldn't wait to tell the girls about this.

When Diandra returned to the room, Mason had moved to sit in the chair beside the window. She took in his fresh Timbs, the wife beater, and his dark blue jeans. There was something about that thug in a nigga that she loved. She loved that tough street edge that Seven just didn't have. Seven was a good provider, very loving, but sometimes too smothering. Too loving.

She was nuts.

"Yeah," Mason said as he placed his hand over his crotch. "I know you want this."

He was right. She did. "Damn right I do."

Fuck it! She was gonna sleep with him tonight. Just one last time and then it would be done.

She moved towards him, slowly removing her clothes. He just sat there and watched her. His body was growing harder. He loved her. That's why he had stopped seeing all his other shorties for her. That's why he was there. He had to persuade her not to marry old dude.

She watched him unzip his pants and pull himself out, stroking his thickness. She licked her lips as she looked at him. There were no flowery words of love as there were with Seven. Instead there was this intense burning that needed to be quenched. She needed him inside her and fast.

As he continued to stroke himself, she got down on her hands and knees and crawled towards him. She stopped when she got between his legs and replaced his hand with her mouth. She licked him up and down his shaft.

He gripped the back of her head forcing him deeper into her mouth. She had always liked it a little rough. Seven was always gentle when she went down on him.

She pulled her mouth away from him and climbed to his face. She sat there, waiting for his tongue to caress her body. She was not disappointed. His mouth latched onto her clit, sucking and pulling like she liked it. He swept around her outer lips, before entering her. She held onto the back of his head, riding his face until she came.

He picked her up and dropped her on the bed. He shrugged out of his clothes and landed beside her on the bed. No words were exchanged. Mason moved on top of her and with one knee spread her legs open. He placed his body at her center and could feel the heat coming from her. It made him harder.

Diandra's eyes never once left his as she felt him moving inside her. She thrust her body upwards to meet him thrust for thrust. She could feel his body tighten inside her. His strokes became faster and his breathing labored. She knew that he was coming. However, she wasn't prepared for his next words.

"I love you girl. I gave up my shorties for you."

She continued to move her body until she came. Mason hugged her tight to him as she climaxed. Once her body calmed down, she wrenched out of his arms.

"What did you say?"

"You heard me. I love you. You can't marry Seven. Not after what just happened."

"Are you serious? What just happened was a fuck. A one last time type of thing."

Diandra eyed the play of emotions over Mason's face. Damn, she could see she had hurt his feelings, but she couldn't dwell on that.

"You're talking like a buster. I suggest you get dressed and go get one of your shorties, because I'm marrying Seven."

Mason rolled out of the bed to his feet and turned his back to her. Reaching down for his clothes he slid into his pants and shirt

He turned to face her.

"We'll see about that," he said.

"What do you mean?"

"Nuthing shorty, just talking out the side of my neck. But remember what I said. When you least expect it...."

With that as his parting shot he turned and walked out the room.

Diandra didn't know what do. What if he showed up and tried to stop the wedding? What if he told Seven? All the what ifs played in her mind. Got dammit she had fucked up again. However, she was gonna be on her toes.

Seven may not sling the dick like Mason. He may not have that thuggish swagger, but he had security and that was the most important thing. She had a man that could take care of her on long money. Not that short ass drug money Mason had.

Kendra woke with a start, pressing a hand to her abdomen. She had been having minor cramps for the past three days.

Count, Kendra! She said to herself as she rolled from side to side.

Her movements rose Niall. Wiping the sleep from his eyes he noticed her holding her stomach while moaning in pain. Panicking, he jumped to his knees.

"Kendra! What's wrong, baby?"

"N...N...Niall- something's wrong." She had overdone it. She shouldn't have danced so much last night at the Bachelorette party.

As she rolled to her side again, his eyes noted her bloody nightgown and the blood stained sheets.

"Oh my God!" he yelled holding his hand to his head in distress. He didn't want to say anything, but that damn party she went to last night could have triggered this.

"Call the doctor." She moaned again. *I'm losing the baby,* she silently repeated to herself.

Niall had to calm himself down. *Something was wrong with the baby,* he thought. Quickly turning, he grabbed the phone from the nightstand and punched the number to her doctor.

Panic was rioting within him. "Yes this is Niall Adams! I need to talk to Dr. Peoples! Its an emergency!"

"I'm sorry sir, this is Dr. People's answering service. Can I get your name, the name of the patient and the nature of your emergency?"

"I don't have time for all these questions!" he roared into the phone. "My fiancée is pregnant. She's bleeding and doubled over in pain. Her name is Kendra Thompson."

"Calm down, sir. What is your number?"

Niall gave the woman the number as he pulled on his sweats. "443-555-1134...I'm taking her to the emergency room."

Disconnecting the call, he moved over to Kendra, wrapping her up in the duvet from the bed.

He ran down the steps with her in his arms, swooped up his keys from the tray in the hall and hit the remote start to his truck. He slid her into the back seat, slammed the door and hopped into his seat putting the vehicle in motion before closing his door.

He made his way to Harris General Hospital in record time, pulling into the emergency spot reserved for police officers. He ignored the man yelling at him to move his car as he placed Kendra in his arms, running through the emergency room doors.

"My fiancée is pregnant and bleeding," he told the nurse at the reception desk. She looked ready to refuse him service as he jumped ahead of the others standing before her.

He pulled the duvet away from Kendra's middle to show her the bloody nightdress.

"Right this way, sir," she said, moving into the triage area.

"Who is her doctor?"

"Dr. Peoples. I've already called and left a message with her answering service. I can't wait for her. Kendra needs help *now*!"

"Sir, calm down, please. You'll only put your fiancée in further distress. We need her to calm down and not panic," she said to him as he helped her to place Kendra on the bed.

They immediately began to take her vitals, pushing him to the background. He felt helpless and lost. That was his entire future there on that bed and he couldn't do a damn thing to help.

"Sir if you could just wait outside, please? We will contact you when we have her stabilized."

All he said was, "I'm staying."

"Fine, but you'll have to wait outside."

As the triage nurse showed him to a seat outside Kendra's room, his cell phone rang.

"Niall Adams."

"Mr. Adams, this is Dr. Peoples."

"Thank God. I had to bring Kendra into the emergency room. She woke up in pain and there was blood on the sheets and her nightdress."

"I'm on my way to the hospital now."

"Doc, level with me. Is something going on with the baby?"

His statement was met with a moment of silence.

"Now Mr. Adams, I cannot make a complete diagnosis over the phone. Just try to remain calm and I will have answers for you when I see Kendra."

Before he could object to her answer, the doctor had cut the call.

He was lost. *Should I call her girls?* Just as he picked up his cell to contact Benét, he heard a scream come from behind him. In a flash, he was in the room beside Kendra.

"Baby it's all right" he said. "I'm here and Dr. Peoples is on her way," he said in a calming voice while taking her hand in his.

"Th...the baby-?" she wailed. "I can't lose our baby."

The tears streaming down her face tore at his heart. He was helpless standing there unable to do anything.

"You have to save our baby!" he implored as Dr. Peoples walked through the door. She immediately went to the triage nurse, and then turned to him.

"Mr. Adams, I am going to have to insist that you wait outside."

Without waiting for him to answer she began giving instructions to the team of medics in the room. Dr. Peoples' face turned serious as she began to examine Kendra, while throwing out orders as she attempted to soothe Kendra's harassed state.

The door closed behind him with a thud of finality. He watched helplessly through the window as a feeling of dread settled in his gut.

S haeyla Andrews rushed from her patio to the sound of her cell phone ringing. Being the type "A" personality that she was, she had programmed her phone to have specific rings for specific people. This number was obviously not programmed in her phone because she could tell by the ring.

Glancing down to the bouncing, purple flashes of her display, she recognized the number, a number that had lain at the fringes of her mind for the past few months. Try as she might she couldn't get him or the extremely humiliating way he treated her out of her mind, yet the sight of his number made her heart skip. Her palms became damp and beads of sweat broke out on her forehead.

She knew deep in her heart that it was never going to work out for the two of them so why was she tripping over seeing his number flashing on her cell?

"Hello?" she said hesitantly into the phone. Her heart racing. Her memories of him were clear.

He answered with his usual arrogance, "Took you long enough."

"What do you want?"

"I want to see you."

"See me? I don't hear from you for months and you call expecting me to jump at your command to see you?"

"Yes. I know you want to. You know you want to. I'm in your mind; that we both know. Stop playing games and meet me at the penthouse at nine," he said and then hung up.

Shaeyla stared at the phone in her hand. "Damn! Why does he continue to have this affect on me?" she asked herself.

No one knew how many times she had picked up her phone to call him to explain his behavior but she never did. Besides, her girls would kick the living shit out of her ass. Shaeyla didn't know what her problem was. How dare he call her and expect her to run to him? *You know you want to.* His words bounced around in her head. All the humiliation, all the pain he had inflicted on her in the past didn't stop the feeling she had for him. *"In spite of her best effort of forgetting him, she always had the question of, 'What if'?"*

The conversation wore on her mind conflicted with desire and disgust. Moving into her kitchen, she opened her wine cellar and retrieved a bottle of Merlot. The first sip of the ruby liquid calmed her frayed nerves. She immediately downed that glass, and poured another. By the third glass of wine, she had persuaded herself to see him. The alcohol had removed all doubts about seeing him. Like an automaton, she dressed in a slinky jade green sheath dress. The sexy underwear matched perfectly. Subconsciously she knew that Mitch liked matching lingerie...she dressed for him. Tonight was for her. Tonight was a night she needed.

Thoughts of Solomon danced in her head, but she shoved them away. He was confused, didn't know his feelings. Well, she knew hers. She was confused too. Before that thought could sink into the nether recesses of her mind, she eyed herself one last time in the mirror and headed to her car and to Mitch.

•••••

As she parked in the underground parking lot in his building, she placed a calming hand to her stomach. *Why are you doing this?* Her subconscious asked her. *You feel something wrong. You know you do.* She rubbed her hands over her face, checked her image in the mirror and exited the car.

Her mind wondered what he had planned for the evening as she rode the elevator to the penthouse. She heard jazz playing in the background as the doors opened. She glanced around the room until her eyes rested on his form lounging against the fireplace. He was dressed in his signature black, looking menacing yet sophisticated.

"I knew you would come," he said as he sauntered to her. He took in her appearance. "You look beautiful. That color suits you, wear it more often for me."

Shaeyla stepped back. "What do you want from me, Mitch? Why am I even here?"

Walking to his bar he smiled, and then turned to her, "You're here because this is where you want to be."

He poured her a glass of red wine. Carefully he studied her as he walked to hand her the glass.

"Why did you come?"

She didn't really need anymore to drink, but her mouth was suddenly dry. Taking a sip of the wine she turned to view the panoramic view of the Inner Harbor.

Walking up behind her, he placed a hand to the small of her back and whispered, "You came because you wanted to." He turned her around, "You came because you had to. Because of this." His mouth melded into hers. Automatically her tongue sought his. *This is Shaeyla.*

He moved them up the stairs and into his bedroom. Her body responded to his unconsciously. He undressed her slowly, talking to her. He could sense her nerves. He knew that she wanted to stop. That she didn't want to be here. He knew Shaeyla better than she knew herself. But hell, she could suck a mean dick. She made him feel things when she did that. He hasn't been able to find another woman that could perform oral like that. He also wanted to see how far he could take her sexually. He knew that he had her mind, and getting a woman's mind is half the battle. He would find out tonight and prove to Solomon that once his woman always his woman.

Shaeyla was beyond thinking. She anticipated the feel of his solid dark body hovering over. Her body was at a completely heightened state of awareness. She didn't object to his blindfolding her. She didn't object to the feeling of his tongue lathing her body as he laid her on the sheets. He pulled her on top of him as he turned to his back, his urgings to sit on his face sending a ripple of sensation down her spine. A feeling of erotic awareness bubbled inside her as he tightened the blindfold over her eyes.

She suddenly heard a door open then close and foot-falls along the hallway, which led to his master suite. She could hear something fall to the floor, but she was so caught up in the rapture of his tongue lathing and strok-ing him that she ignored the voice inside her head telling her *Someone's in the room!*

Instead, she rode his face not missing a beat making sure he didn't lose a drop of her essence. She felt finger-nails trail along her spine.

"*A woman,*" her mind screamed out as she moved to lift herself from his face. Almost as if he knew her reac-tion, he clamped his arms around her slick thighs render-ing her powerless to his sensual onslaught. A huge lump formed in her throat stifling her protests.

"*No!*" she wanted to scream. "*Stop, this is not what I want!*"

With the blindfold over her eyes, she had to rely on her other senses. Her hearing alerted her to the sound of paper tearing, then movement from behind her as sheets rustled. She feels him move as if to accommodate some-one. Then he begins to move and the person begins to moan softly almost as if she was told to stifle her cries of delight.

He commanded the "woman" to touch, lick, stroke, and caress Shaeyla's body before turning his voice in Shaeyla's direction willing her to participate. Reluctantly her hand lifts to fondle the body of the unknown woman and as she does this woman slowly traces her hand along Shaeyla's arm and around to her back. Shaeyla did not want to participate but she was powerless. Shaeyla became caught up in his soothing voice urging her to touch her.

"See, that wasn't so bad," he said in his well-modulated voice.

She was hypnotized and mesmerized by the sensations flowing through her body. *Her girls must never find out that she did this. She must take this to her grave.* Mitch placed his hand on the back of her head pressing her forward as he instructed her to trace his mouth with her tongue. Their tongues dueled, twisting and thrusting in and out in an erotic dance. That's when she felt the heat as another mouth joined in their dance, creating a triangle of tongues and mouths. *And then there were two,* as the woman pressed her mouth on Shaeyla's. Mitch suckled on Shaeyla's breast to distract her as the woman began to rain kisses from her back to the base of her spine while her hand urged her forward onto her knees.

Effortlessly, her legs spread and she pushed her ass into the air granting access to her hot core. She couldn't believe the anticipation she felt at having a woman about to do that which only a man has ever done. The tentative strokes from her tongue around her center and the feel of it enter her, made her jerk. Instinctively, she pressed herself backward into the mouth that was giving her pleasure.

She didn't notice that Mitch had stopped his ministrations of her breast and eased out from under her to watch the women enjoy each other.

Then she felt his hands on her head as he moved to untie the blindfold.

"I want you to see what I see. See how turned on I am by the pleasure she is giving you," he told her. Her eyes dropped to his middle where it appeared that he grew and swell even larger before her eyes. He moved the woman from her and entered Shaeyla with long deep thrusts that brought them to a mind-blowing climax. She forgot about the woman as he turned her into his arms, his whispers of gratification lulling her to sleep.

She awoke in the middle of the night with Mitch wrapped around her body and the other woman wrapped around him. She eased herself away from him, found her clothes and dressed as hot tears poured down her face. Her hands were trembling too much for her to button her blouse, so she grabbed it together, turned from the room, and ran to the elevator and out the door to her car.

As she sat behind the wheel she placed her head on the steering wheel stunned, dazed, and confused about her actions of the night before. She had to talk to someone. Her mind instantly went to Benét, and starting her car. She backed out of her space determined to get the guilt off her chest.

Halfway there she knew that she could never tell her girls what she did. Fearfully, she began to shake from the frightening images in her mind. *"You what?" "That's nasty!" Your ass is a freak!"* The thoughts swirling in Shaeyla's mind at what she thought her girls would say about her made her sick.

She suddenly stopped in the middle of the road, *"Oh my God, Solomon can never find out about this!"*

Benét threw back the covers and padded over to her window to see who was banging on her door. The sight of the pearl colored G35 coupe had her stepping into her shoes and throwing on her silk robe to answer the door.

"What in the world is Shaeyla doing here at this time of the morning?" she asked herself. Her mind immediately went to Worthy. Something had to be wrong. Turning to see if Christian was still sleeping, she eased open her bedroom door and headed down the stairs.

Throwing open the door, she took in Shaeyla's unbuttoned blouse and tear-streaked face. A sense of déjà vu came over Benét because this scene was the exact opposite of what happened to her last year.

"Shaeyla, what's wrong?"

"Benét, I have made the biggest mistake of my life," she sobbed.

"Come inside and tell me what's going on."

Benét steered her into the living room as she looked up the stairs to make sure that Shaeyla's crying did not wake Christian. The last thing that she needed was for him to come down the stairs, stirring up more questions.

Sitting Shaeyla down she sat beside her. "Now tell me what is wrong. Is everything okay with Solomon?"

The mention of Solomon pushed Shaeyla into more despair.

"I...I...I...fu-fucked up. I slept with Mitch last night," she told her friend, leaving out any mention of a third party, a woman, being involved.

"What?" Shaeyla, what the fuck is up with you and Mitch? Does this nigga have a gold dick or something? Damn! What about Solomon? Or have you forgotten about him?"

"No, I don't know Benét, don't yell at me. I feel bad enough as it is. But there is something about Mitchell Steele that I can't let go. I don't know if it's a jones in my bones, love, lust, or what. He has this hold over me that I can't control. All I know is that he calls and I go running."

Benét stood with her hands on her hips, shaking her head in disgust at Shaeyla. She had no idea what her girl thought. Mitch was not the man for her, but she was right in saying he had some kind of hold over her. In a way she understood, because isn't that what Christian had over her and vice versa? Shit, here she was chastising Shaeyla's ass when she was just as, if not more confused her damn self.

"I don't know what I'm going to do."

"I tell you what you're going to do. You're going to put it behind you. You have to."

"I have to tell Solomon."

"No- that's the last thing that you should do. Brothers can't handle that shit. No, no, you need to keep this shit right here on the low. Are you going to tell Kendra, Diandra, and Worthy?"

"I don't see why not, we tell each other everything else."

Benét thought of her friend's words and felt a sense of guilt since she was hiding her relationship with Christian. Just then a sound from upstairs made both women's heads pop up.

"Are the kids here?" Shaeyla asked as she stood to straighten out her clothes and swipe her hands over her face.

"Uh...no," Benét said hesitantly. *Damn...think Benét-think!*

Shaeyla's head cocked to the side. "Ooohhhh...girl, when did you and Kenny get back together?"

"Uh...its not Kenny."

"Well if its not Kenny, then who..." the questions stopped as realization dawned that if it wasn't the kids or Kenny then it had to be- "Girl don't even tell me that Christian is upstairs."

Benét turned away from the scowl on her friends face. Twisting her hands she gave her girl a placating smile.

"I know it looks bad, but it just happened."

"What do you mean it just happened? It wasn't but a month ago when school started and now here the two of you are fucking again."

• • • • •

Christian awakened when he rolled over searching for Benét only to find that he was in bed alone. Getting up to check the bathroom, he pulled on his pants, zipping but not fastening the clasp, exposing his hard chest and a forest of black curls that disappeared beneath them. He was met with the sound of raised voices coming from below as he opened the door. Following the voices he walked into the living room and answered the question Shaeyla had asked of Benét.

"Yes, we are," he answered in a cool and disapproving tone.

Both ladies turned at the sound of his voice. He could see that they were surprised.

With the mood that Shaeyla was in, Benét became apprehensive at the confrontation she sensed brewing between her friend and her lover.

Holding his hand out, she trustingly placed hers in his as he drew her into his side. Lovingly, he placed a kiss on her brow his eyes never once leaving that of her friend. He could see the derision within them almost as if she was searching for genuineness.

"Well...I'm out, Benét, call me later," said Shaeyla, releasing a heavy sigh.

"Listen Shaeyla, don't leave like this. Let me explain what's going on."

"No...No, there is no need to explain. I see that you have what you want, or at least what you think you want. Besides it's none of my business."

"True, it is none of your business, but-"

"But what? *But oh I'm trying to get back with my husband*" Shaeyla asked her friend throwing their prior conversation back at her. "Remember those words you told me before starting back at school?"

Benét's anxiety level elevated. "Yes, dammit! I remember the words! You didn't have to remind me, but...but"...

Her voice stilled because she didn't know how to answer Shaeyla without sounding like a hypocrite. Hell, she was a hypocrite for it was only mere minutes ago when she had voiced her displeasure at Shaeyla's sleeping with Mitch again.

"But somehow I fell on Christian's dick *again*! Is that what you were going to say?" Shaeyla threw over her shoulder as she began to walk from the room. She'd had enough of Benét's hypocritical bullshit.

"Let's not talk about falling on a dick, girlfriend, because your ass is stuck on one your got damn self!"

Benét's words stopped her in her tracks and she turned a scornful eye to her friend.

"You know what? I'm going, before we both say things that we'll regret."

Christian stepped forward to say something, but Benét held him back. He felt the hurt that both women had inflicted on each other, and he was part of the reason. He saw Benét's head drop. Her shoulders shook as her body was wracked with tears. He cradled her in his arms, pulling her onto his lap as he let the tears relieve her anguish. He knew that her girlfriends meant a lot to her.

His coolly controlled voice consoled her, as he rocked her trembling form to calmness. He didn't know whether it was hours or minutes later, but finally her tears subsided as she drifted into a fretful slumber.

S eeing Solomon with his ex did something to her. It made her realize that she needed to leave, both he and Mitch alone. Shaeyla continued to refuse his phone calls at home and in the office. When he called her cell number, she placed the calls on ignore. Eventually, he would get the hint that she wasn't trying to listen to his bullshit. As her phone rang, she absent-mindedly picked up without checking to see who it was.

"Shaeyla Andrews."

"Finally," Solomon's voice said into the receiver.

Before she could respond her doorbell rang.

"Hold on," she told him as she walked to the door.

She looked from him to the phone and back again. "W... What-W-Why...? What are you doing here Solomon?", her voice faltered as she stepped back into her home.

Her eyes drank from the sight of him. Her heart raced. Gathering herself, her brow wrinkled.

"Shaeyla please let me explain."

"I've told you that I don't want to hear your explanation."

"Dammit! You have to listen to me!" his voice roared. He grabbed her by the arm and forced her onto her couch. Towering over her, his chest heaved with emotion.

"What Solomon? What can you tell me or explain to me that will make me understand? You're no better than your boy."

"Don't ever compare me to Mitch. Ever, do you understand? If you shut up long enough to listen to me -- I didn't know Vanessa was even back in town. Dammit, when we broke up, she moved out west and that was it."

Shaeyla snorted her disbelief. "Yeah right."

"That is right. I am a one-woman man, Shaeyla."

"Why did she come to see you? What were the two of you arguing about?" Shaeyla's questions bombarded him. "Who broke it off?"

"Slow down and listen to what I have to say."

"I'm listening."

"Vanessa and I were together for seven years. I wanted to marry her, but she wanted a career. End of story. I can't lie and say that I didn't try to get back with her, because I did. However, she never wanted to get back with me. Until now."

"And --"

"And to be honest -- my feelings for her are just as confusing as my feelings for you. I know that is not what you wanted to hear. She is here looking for a place because she asked for a transfer."

"What do you want from me, Solomon? Do you want me to make it easy for you?"

"No. I want you to understand that I am going to need some time to sort out my feelings."

"Okay, take all the time you need. Just understand that I am not going to wait around hoping that you'll choose me."

Solomon arrived in the office early, yet it still wasn't early enough to beat Mitch. Since he had warned Mitch about disrespecting Shaeyla, their conversations over the last month had been tenuous at best. He dreaded talking to him, but he couldn't get to his corner office without passing by Mitch.

As he walked up to Mitch's door, he set his mind on business. With a short rap on the doorframe, he stepped over the threshold and into Mitch's inner sanctum.

The cool blue tones were the perfect backdrop for the various paintings that represented the African Diaspora. The softly muted gray-brushed suede chairs flanked his desk and that was where Solomon planted himself.

Mitch eyed the grim set of Solomon's mouth, his tight closed-in expression, and covertly smiled.

"Morning. What's up?"

The heavy sigh left Solomon and before he knew it, the events of the past couple of days poured out of him.

As Mitch listened, he was thrilled at the thought of Shaeyla rejecting Solomon, yet disturbed at the indecisiveness of his friend.

"So Vanessa is back and now you're confused?"

"Yeah. Crazy isn't it."

"Didn't you just tell me not to hurt Shaeyla anymore,

yet you turn around and do the same thing?" Mitch exploded. "Now I understand why she was crying."

This peaked Solomon's interest. "What do you mean crying? When did you see Shaeyla?" he questioned.

"The same day she saw you and Vanessa in the parking lot."

"Dammit, Mitch! I told you to stay away from Shaeyla."

"No! You told me not to disrespect her in the future. You told me not to call her out of her name. But you didn't tell me to stay away from her."

Solomon heard something in Mitch's voice. "Are you saying you're going to try to get her back?"

"That's exactly what I'm saying."

"What about your fiancée?"

"A minor detail that has been corrected. See, my friend, I am now free, which is imminently more than you can say. Besides bruh, I know your history with Vanessa. She has always been a fever in your blood...one you've had trouble shaking. If she wasn't, there wouldn't be any question in your mind about your feelings for Shaeyla."

Solomon silently acknowledged that Mitch was correct. He had hurt Shaeyla and he was torn. The thought of her back in the arms of Mitch and his free wheeling views on sex was disturbing. Mitch was adventurous. Didn't mind twosomes, threesomes and foursomes, and had apparently opened Shaeyla up to new experiences as she was very adventurous and giving in her lovemaking.

"Listen. Our friendship has withstood a lot. I stand by

my words on not hurting Shaeyla, it's just that I feel I'm not the man she needs right now."

"I'm glad we agree."

"Wait, Mitch. I don't think that you're the kind of man she needs either. Hell, you completely devastated her at the ball. Lord knows what other humiliating acts you've put her through to prove her loyalty to you. Let's give her a month to adjust."

"A month to adjust to what? Another brother?"

"Whatever, but right now I think she needs space from both of us."

Mitch turned to look out of his window at the view of the Inner Harbor. Deep down, he knew what Solomon said was correct, but he couldn't take the chance on another brother scooping her up. Flashes of that night flashed through his mind. That green dress. The blindfold. *What Sol doesn't know, won't hurt him.* If she thought he had pursued her in the past, his pursuit of her was now going to leave her breathless and wondering Solomon who?

"Alright! Deal. I will give her one month, but after that all bets are off," Mitchell told him as they shook hands to seal the pact.

Solomon immediately called Vanessa as he entered his office. He wanted to talk to her on his turf, so he was inviting her to his home for dinner. Who was he fooling? Mitch was right. For the first two years after she left, he had begged and pleaded for her to come back to him. All for naught. She was dedicated to her career and nothing he said or did would deter her. Not even when he asked her to marry him did she waver. Here she was four years later, more beautiful than ever, and tethering his emotions in knots.

His thoughts turned to Shaeyla. She was a fantastic woman who had come into his life to fill a void of emptiness and loneliness. He enjoyed the conversation they shared. The hot lovemaking and inventive ways she had for turning him on. He especially loved the way she went down on him though she was careful never to let him release himself in her mouth. *Which brought him full circle to Vanessa.* Vanessa had cast a spell on him seven years ago, capturing his heart, body, mind and soul.

His feelings towards Vanessa had been repressed. He thought that he had successfully banished them, and he had believed that Shaeyla had played a part in his healing, but she hadn't. Her zaniness was a Band-Aid to his broken heart. Her spontaneity intrigued him. So much so, that he had believed himself Vanessa-free. When, in reality, he had merely suppressed his feelings of love for Vanessa, transferring them into lust for Shaeyla. Lust he had almost convinced himself was love.

The best thing for him to do was to call Shaeyla and tell her face-to-face of his decision.

His attempts to contact her at home and on her cell were futile. When he tried the office Bilal informed him she was on her way to his office to complete the plans for their corporate retreat. Confused because he didn't remember seeing her in his day planner, he contacted his secretary who advised that she was meeting with Mitch.

Why did his body reject thoughts of them? Is it because he knew Mitch and knew that he wasn't going to wait the month they had agreed on, rather he was going to begin his subtle campaign of seduction? Whatever his friend was up to, he didn't like, but how could he in all honesty question his friend on a woman he had just a minute ago decided was not the woman for him? Confusion did not sit well with Solomon for he prided himself on his manliness. On being a thorough brother. Instead of the indecisive person that he had become. *Damn! At 41, I should be more together.*

• • • • •

Shaeyla slid into the empty parking slot closest to the entrance of Jackson-Steele. She had not seen either of the owners since her tryst with Mitchell. Funny how it seemed like ages, but in reality, was only a couple of weeks. The silence from the two men worried her. It gave her a false sense of being, as if something large was looming ahead.

Gathering her items from her car, she straightened and turned towards the glass-encased doors. On entering the posh foyer, the receptionist, used to seeing her, pointed her in the direction of the executive offices.

Hmmm, so the gossip hasn't gotten around to the fact that she wasn't seeing Solomon anymore. Interesting. This should make for a very interesting meeting.

Shaeyla glided through the elevator doors, straightened her casually elegant pantsuit and talked herself into remaining calm.

As the elevator doors opened, she walked through and headed directly for Mitchell's office. She had decided to discuss the upcoming events with him. In the future, she would delegate the account to Bilal, playing a minor role in the decisions for Jackson-Steele.

His assistant was nowhere in sight, forcing her to announce herself. Firmly knocking on the door, he barked out "Come."

She rolled her eyes in her head at his lordly command. *"Come"*. Talk about self-absorbed. A noise from the next office stopped her. She turned to find Solomon stepping from his office and with him the woman she knew to be Vanessa.

They both stopped in their tracks, their smiles of joy, wiped away by the tension suddenly permeating the air. The pair of them rooted Shaeyla to the spot. She didn't hear Mitch yell, "It's open." She didn't hear him wrench open his door. All she saw was Solomon looking happier than she'd ever seen him and knew in her heart that she had never loved him. She liked him intensely. She enjoyed his company and knew he would make some woman a wonderful husband. Judging from the gleam in his eyes she knew that woman to be Vanessa.

Solomon cleared his throat. "Hello Shaeyla." Inclining his head, he looked past her. "Mitch".

That's when she felt Mitch's hand on her shoulder. The feeling was surreal. Both men had hurt her and both had comforted her when the other had let her down. Now here she was again in the same situation. Yet, Mitch's hand felt more than comforting. It felt loving. *Or is it wishful thinking?*

Finding her voice, she spoke politely to both of them, and then placed her hand over Mitch's shoulder to show Solomon that she was okay.

As the couple bade them farewell, Mitch steered her into his office. Seating her on his settee, he turned to his liquor cabinet and poured her a brandy.

"Here drink this."

She looked up at him and took the tumbler from his hands downing the brown liquid in one gulp.

"Thanks. I needed that."

Mitchell said nothing. Instead he stood above her holding the empty glass in his hand looking at her. Finally, his voice cut across the silence.

"Are you okay?"

Shaeyla, somewhat chagrined, said, "Yes, believe it or not, I am okay. Thank you for --."

Waving her off, he sat the glass on the drinks cart and leaned on his desk.

"No need to thank me. I know it was -- awkward, but better to have it happen now."

"Yes, I suppose you're right."

Shaking off the moment, she grabbed her briefcase and retrieved the folder of information she had prepared for him.

"This is a detailed proposal for the initial public offering conference."

"Thanks. Solomon and I will review it and get back to you."

"No. Going forward you will work with my assistant on this. I have prior engagements that I am unable to delegate."

"That is not possible," Mitch stated. "I want you on this project."

"Honestly, were it not for business, I would not see either of you." Gathering her things, she added, "Bilal will not decide without me, it's just that he will now be your point of contact."

It was rash on her part to dismiss him, but she had to leave before she lost her self-control. She had shed her last tear over this partnership.

Mitch mulled over her words. He looked at her and realized that she looked tired. There were telltale signs of bags under her eyes. Last year, not to mention the last few weeks had stressed her. He could give her some time, but not a lot.

"Understood."

That was too easy, Shaeyla thought. He was probably

up to something, but she was tired of dealing with her roller coaster emotions when it came to him, so she let it past. She rose from her seat.

"Thank you Mitch. Bilal won't let you down."

Gathering her belongings, he watched her leave. He sat down at his desk and put his plan into action. He had a woman to seduce, but first he had to regain her trust.

Now where did that come from? He asked himself. Granted that he had hurt her in the past, but she was as much at fault as he. He told her from the beginning that he only wanted a casual relationship. Was it his fault that she had convinced herself that their relationship was something more than it was? He told her he wasn't interested in marriage.

So what do you hope to gain by pursuing her again? His conscience asked. *Control.*

Wow! Shaeyla's mind continued to replay her past mistakes. The arrival of the bouquet of hothouse flowers thrust her back in time.

Sunday morning in the bustling diner on the corner of South Street was where Shaeyla found herself waiting for Mitch to join her for breakfast. The waitress painted eyebrows and silvery blue eye shadow were clashing with her see through skin. The jangling bell over the door alerted the patrons to new customers entering the establishment.

Each time the bell rang Shaeyla looked up out of sheer curiosity. She loved to watch the people of Baltimore as they set about their day. She watched as an elderly couple came in and were greeted by the waitress. The bell rang again and as she turned her head to the door she got the shock of her life.

There, holding the door open was Mitchell Steele and that woman. There was an intimacy between them that she thought he only used for her. The sight of them together as he held the door for her made Shaeyla's teeth ache. As he began to seat them his eyes rested on her blanched expression. He leaned down to say something to his companion and they both headed in her direction. He didn't even blink as he calmly walked towards her with the female in tow. Her stomach dropped. Her eyes dilated as the tears tried to push their way out. Blinking her eyes rapidly so as not to break down, her mind reeled as he approached.

As he stopped beside her chair, he leaned down to buss her cheek with his lips. She pulled back. Her eyes questioned his arrogance.

A smirk crossed his handsome face. He introduced the two women to each other. "Shaeyla, this is Diamond. Diamond this is Shaeyla. I figured it was time the two of you met."

With that said he sat down opposite her. He acted so natural and cool like there wasn't a problem in the world. Shaeyla couldn't believe it. She noted that Diamond was not surprised to see her. The moment in it self shocked Shaeyla. Their nonchalance amazed her. How dare he bring a woman with him then have the nerve to introduce her!

She watched as he picked up the menu in front of him and gave one to Diamond. Shaeyla's hand began to shake uncontrollably. She could barely hold her hand steady enough to pick up her coffee. What was she supposed to do? She had heard about men who let the women in their lives know about one another. Yet her cocky-attitude lulled her into adopting the 'can't happen to me' attitude. She just knew that all the shit talking that Mitch did was just words. She didn't believe that he whole-heartedly lived and believed half of the shit he said.

Her girls had told her she didn't believe shit stunk until she smelled it. She smelled it and the odor was as rancid and dank as the real thing.

Quietly she sat there as they ordered. Silently the three of them ate, while Shaeyla snuck furtive glances at the other woman. The competition. Mitch's lover. Her feelings of inadequacy, loneliness, and humiliation appeared to her to be broadcast on the airwaves of the oldies radio station playing in the background. She drank multiple cups of coffee to quell the roiling sensation in her stomach.

She watched as Mitch dabbed the corners of Diamond's mouth. The nausea rose up in her throat at the sight of him catering to her.

"Oh my god! I'm going to throw up," she said in a choked voice.

Mitch turned to her and let out a long audible breath as he stated, "Turn the other way".

Jumping to her feet, she ran to the ladies room, spewing the contents of her stomach into the sink. As she ran the water to rinse her mouth, the door opened to admit Diamond.

Shaeyla continued to wipe her face.

"What?"

The one word showed her annoyance at the intrusion and to her presence.

"You didn't know about me, did you?"

"Obviously not. How long have you known him?"

"Does it matter?"

Shaeyla ignored her question. "Do you have feelings for him?"

"Yes, I do. I can tell that you do also."

"Yes, I do," Shaeyla answered annoyed at the transparency of her feelings. "But I'm taking myself out of the race."

"There is no race."

"Whatever," Shaeyla stated as she threw the napkin away.

Her hand was on the handle of the door as Diamond spoke up. "I'm sorry. I didn't know you felt for him the way you do. We are just friends. I've been married before and I'm not trying to get serious with him, but I can tell that you are."

"Yeah well you're a better woman than me because I have to be the only woman in a man's life."

Opening the door, not caring whether the other woman was behind her or not Shaeyla returned to her seat.

Grabbing her purse, she retrieved her wallet and pulled out some money to cover her meal. Mitch never once looked up from his plate as he asked if she was leaving.

"Yes, I'm gone. I love myself too much to be the third wheel in this act."

"Stop it with the fucking dramatics. At least I was honest with you. I never lied to you about the standing of our relationship. You allowed yourself to assume that because I spent time with you that we were exclusive. That was your mistake. Diamond understands that, and I respect her for that. So deal with it and keep it moving."

Her humiliation increased tenfold. She could hear the silence of the patrons as Mitch's voice boomed throughout the small diner. *The snickering and tittering lanced her composure.*

There was a swell of emotion imminent, turning, she ran as if the devil himself was after her.

What a fool she'd been over Mitch. She couldn't judge men and didn't have the will to fight anymore. As she walked into her kitchen, she decided to throw herself into what she should've been doing in the first place- that of planning the weddings of her best friends. For some reason she couldn't settle down. Instead of placing the flowers in a vase, she left them in the box.

What was Mitch up to? The card read to a new beginning. A new beginning for what? Them?

He confused her. Shaeyla knew one thing and that was that he could forget them ever getting together again. Just put the last few weeks down to her stupidity. *Again! Damn girl, when will you learn to stop putting yourself in one-sided situations?*

She stepped over to her wine cooler, removed a bottle of merlot and poured herself a glass. Sitting in her favorite chair her thoughts again turned to Mitchell and Solomon. Her mind kept going back to the past months of emotional turmoil.

Hell maybe, I'm just not good enough for any man. She thought. *Then again, maybe they aren't good enough for me.* She drained her glass, crossed over and threw the hothouse flowers in the trash. With determination she began jotting down notes for Diandra's wedding, promising to plan an event Baltimore wouldn't soon forget.

FRESH STARTS

S haeyla arrived at the hotel where Diandra and the girls had stayed the night before. She chose not to stay because she had plans to see Mitchell after the rehearsal dinner and didn't want to hear any shit about what or whom she saw. They thought her crazy for even considering seeing his trifling ass. It had been two months since her talk with Solomon. He had no words for her either, ever since she started going out with Mitch again. It was his ego. She didn't care. She was going to do what she wanted to do and if Mitchell Steele thought she wasn't going to see other men than he was crazy. She was going to do *her*.

Taking her mind to the forthcoming nuptials she rapped on Diandra's door. The girlish sounds coming from within the suite brought a smile to her face. She knew that they partied last night, because she knew her girl.

Benét's daughter Zaria opened the door.

"Aunty Shaeyla," Zaria squealed, wrapping her in her arms. "This is going to be the best wedding ever."

"Hey!" the ladies yelled in unison.

"Hey y'all! Are we ready to do this thing or what?"

"Girl...these dresses and my gown." Diandra shook her head at the beauty of the garments, speechless. "Baltimore is not ready for me."

"You can say that again. We still have a few details to go over."

"Wait before you start. Michelle is going to do our makeup, then get ready herself. All of us are showered and ready to put on our dresses once that is done."

Shaeyla was impressed.

"Great, her are the flower girls baskets and Seven's ring," she explained to her as she began to drop the bags that she had in her hands. "Here are the bridesmaid's gifts. I have to stop past Seven's to drop off the grooms-men gifts. I will meet you at the church."

A knock came to the door. "Damn, its like grand central station up in here," Diandra exclaimed.

At the door were several waiters with trays and carts covered with savory delights. The headwaiter announced the arrival of brunch, then asked to come in and handed her a card.

They placed the trays on the dining room table and the liveried carts around it before grandly removing the chafing lids. As the headwaiter walked out, he congratu-lated her, bowed graciously and exited. At that moment she remembered the card in her hand, she instantly rec-ognized Seven's distinctive scrawl. Breaking the seal, she opened it with trembling fingers to read.

"Because I love you...Because you're MY everything... Because I cannot wait to make you my wife... I wanted to be the first person to give you something new...I Love You, Seven."

With tears cascading down her face, she turned to see her bridesmaids exclaiming over the lavish dishes before them. There were strawberries, cantaloupe, and honeydew melons, along with an assortment of delectable pastries. The cart held several bottles of Dom Perignon and orange juice for mimosas.

"Girl...thanks so much for getting this for us," came a voice from the back of the room. Her cousin was steadily piling her plate up with the goodies before her.

"Don't thank me." Diandra said as she wiped the tears from her face. "Thank Seven."

"Well why didn't they take the cover off this one?" Zaria asked as she lifted the lid.

"Here Aunt Diandra, this is for you."

Zaria handed her the oblong white velvet box. As she took it, she remembered the last phrase on the card.

"Well open it," Zaria implored.

Flipping the top open she found an exquisite tennis bracelet. The bracelet she had been wanting for her birthday. A one-of-a-kind 6-carat bracelet to match her engagement ring was nestled inside. The bridal party exclaimed over it and how lucky she was to be marrying a man like Seven.

"Yes, I am lucky. Now let's eat and then we have to start preparing ourselves for *MY WEDDING!*"

· · · · ·

Shaeyla smiled as she approached Seven and Diandra's new home. As she rang the bell, she checked her watch and mentally checked off the task on her to-do list. Seven's father opened the door and relieved her of the bags she carried. As Seven descended the steps to his foyer, Shaeyla eyed the boxes waiting to be unpacked. Benét was going to try to get as much decorating done on their home as possible while they honeymooned.

"Shaeyla." Seven greeted her with a warm smile.

"Now that's what I love to see."

"What?"

"A happy man."

"I am happy and blessed that I finally got my girl. Even though she challenged me every step of the way."

"Don't I know it? We kept telling her about you, but she didn't want to hear it. Then you kissed her at the party and she was through."

Seven's smile was infectious. "What's in the bags?"

"Oh- this one contains the groomsmen's gifts. This is for your father and best man, and here is the ring bearer pillow."

"Cool."

"Oh before I forget. The bracelet was stunning and I have to say thank you for loving our girl, thank you for showing her true love, devotion, and commitment."

Seven bowed his head as she reached up to kiss his cheek.

"Now I have to finalize some things at the church. I will see you no later than 3:15."

"I don't know if I can wait that long."

"See you later," Shaeyla called over her shoulder as she left.

Ever since the scare that she and Niall had months back, Kendra was especially careful. Hell, she had to be. After a two- day stint in the hospital, her doctor had placed her on complete bed rest until her delivery date. Niall, bless his heart, was the most attentive man a woman could have, but today she was not going to be coaxed into changing her mind.

Because of her condition, Shaeyla had held Diandra's bridal shower at her home instead of the restaurant that overlooked the harbor. Her girls were also treating her as if she would break. But today, she was not having it. She was going to the wedding regardless. Besides, she had spoken to Dr. Peoples who advised her that she could go for a few hours, but at the first sign of fatigue, she was to leave and get home immediately. She hadn't said anything to Niall about her conversation, but she was going to celebrate at Diandra's wedding, come hell or high water.

Today was also supposed to be her wedding day. The day that she and Niall solidified *their* love for each other and for their child. Due to her delicate condition though, they had to postpone their nuptials until after the baby was born. As if in tune with its mother, she felt a fluttery movement of her child. *I promise that nothing is going to happen to you.* Placing a hand over her protruding belly, she cradled her child within.

Niall caught her as she sat at her vanity table. The scowl on his brow showed his disapproval at the outfit lying on the bed. The pink dress had sequins on the top with a long flowing skirt, which in his opinion was guaranteed to trip her. Stooping down, he picked up the pale pink slides on the floor.

"You're not even thinking of wearing these? Are you?"

Before she had a chance to respond, he replaced them in the closet and pulled out a pair of black flats.

Kendra huffed at his highhandedness but in the end she understood that he was looking out for her. She had to admit to herself that although she loved the attention, he and her girls were beginning to smother her.

With a sigh, she dressed, slid into her shoes and called Niall to come help her to the car. No matter what, she was going to be there for her girl.

Niall eased her up from her vanity chair and slowly proceeded to the door. As they walked outside Kendra took in the beautiful cloudless blue sky and beaming sun with a smile. Today was going to be a glorious day for a wedding.

Once in their car, Niall placed the packages in the trunk. Kendra had gone overboard in the gifts she had gotten for Diandra and Seven, but she wanted them to have the fantastic place setting Diandra had picked out. Besides, Diandra's family couldn't afford half the items on the list, so between her, Benét, and Shaeyla, they had split the most expensive items and purchased them from the registry.

"All set?" Niall asked, breaking into her thoughts.

"Yes. Let's go. I can't wait to see her!"

In the process of buckling his belt, he turned to her. "Are you sure you're okay?"

"Yes, I'm fine."

"Today should have been our day as well..."

Kendra stopped him, "I know, but this is for the best. I don't want this lavish event that Diandra is having. I want something quiet and elegant, with the people who really matter in our lives there," she said leaning over to kiss him.

He eyed her longingly as if in search for the truth. Satisfied as he saw her smile, he straightened in his seat, snapped his belt in place and pointed the car south to the Inner Harbor.

Bliss had broken curfew the night before, so Worthy was in danger of not attending Diandra's wedding. Her thoughts turned nasty.

I swear if Ms. Carter won't let me go, I am going to fuck Bliss up.

She glanced at her watch, knowing without a shadow of a doubt that Benét was picking her up on time. All the arrangements had been made. Because of her stint in rehab, she was unable to be in Diandra's wedding and may not be able to be in Kendra's.

Kendra. Something was definitely going on because both Shaeyla and Benét became evasive when she asked about Kendra. They said she was tired out from the pregnancy but the exchanged glances between the two told her there was more to the story.

Breaking through her thoughts was the loud thumping sound of the director of the center's hard soled shoes along the cement floor.

She wished Amanda was still in charge. She was a lot more personable than this old witch. Ms. Carter appeared before her, stern and haggard. A good piece of dick would remove that sour ass look from her face, thought Worthy as she eyed her.

She took in Worthy's dress. A beautiful soft-shelled

pink concoction designed to entice as well as flirt. The satin bodice had spaghetti straps with hand sewn matching seed pearls that gave way to a fantastic sheer organza skirt, something Worthy never would've gone for. She knew that Shaeyla had enjoyed picking it out for her. She didn't want to disappoint her by not wearing it. Diandra had visited two days ago to deliver the dress and to surprise her with a new hairstyle. It was swept into a beautiful up-do with selected tendrils left out lending a soft romantic look to Worthy's freshly made up face. It was the style that all the women in the wedding were wearing.

Worthy eyed Ms. Carter as she perused her person from head to toe. Her eyes lingered over the dress, pausing at the matching seed pearl shoes and clutch. Worthy almost thought she saw a wistful sigh of envy in Ms. Carter's eyes, but quickly threw that thought out as the black eyes rested on her face.

Oh boy! This bitch looks like she is about to pull the rug from under me.

"Ms. Grier is here for you," she stated with distaste.

I don't know nor care what is going on or even why she hadn't brought up Bliss' faux pas, but I'm hot footing it out of here.

"Thank you Ms. Carter," Worthy said sweetly as she gathered her matching wrap and headed towards the lobby.

Benét turned as she saw several heads turn in the direction of the stairs. Worthy walked down them slowly and at the sight of Benét she ran the rest of the way.

Wrapped in each other's embrace, tears flowed down their faces at the sheer happiness of the day. It would be the first time they would all be together again.

Benét held Worthy away from her. The last time they were here she had noticed how she had put on weight and that her face had lost its sallow complexion, but the hair had still been jacked up. Today she was transformed into a vision. Benét couldn't believe that this was *Worthy.* Shaeyla and her romantic self had placed all the girls in the same color gown but Benét's was off the shoulder, and the skirt was cut on the bias.

"Girl! Look at you! You look fantastic."

Grinning from ear-to-ear Worthy twirled around.

"Don't thank me. Thank Shaeyla. Isn't it beautiful? The problem is I would never have picked this out for myself."

"Come on. Let's go," Benét said, taking her hand. "I can't wait until they see you!" she finished excitedly.

The two women talked excitedly to each other on the drive to the church. Worthy was filling Benét in on the recent events at the center.

"Girl, I almost thought that sour puss Ms. Carter was going to deny me going to the wedding today."

"Deny? How can she deny anything? You can sign yourself in or out, right?"

"Yes, but there are rules to everything. Bliss broke two rules yesterday. She snuck out of the center and then returned after curfew. Hell I've never been to jail, but if your roommate fucks up you fuck up."

"That's a stupid rule to enforce on adults."

"Yeah, I know. But since it's somewhat state funded, they make the rules and I have to follow them. Especially if I ever want to see Jared again."

"He misses you."

"I know. I spoke to my mother the other day. Benét, I am going to get my life right. I promise you that."

Benét listened to Worthy's words. She truly wanted to believe in her friend, but Benét was a realist. She knew how hard it was to kick drugs. She had seen too many loved ones have the same affirmation only to slide back into the seedy world of addiction. Instead of voicing her fears and misgivings she reached out and squeezed Worthy's hand.

"We are here for you."

Minutes later they pulled into the parking lot of the church gathered their belongings and headed inside.

The ride to the church was filled with her and her bridesmaids singing the silliest of songs. As they belted out "Going to the Chapel" Diandra's elated smile radiated throughout the stretch limo. Exiting, she made her way to the bride's anteroom to await her walk down the aisle.

Diandra stared at her reflection in the mirror. She felt a million feelings and emotions. She wanted to run. She wanted to stay. She was in a daze. She felt lightheaded, like she was going to faint and fly at the same time. As her mother strode into the room with tears in her eyes, Diandra turned.

"Here is the handkerchief that your grandmother carried on her wedding day," her mother said.

Mentally going over her bridal checklist, she touched the new bracelet that Seven had given her and watched it sparkle in the light. Then she tucked the old lace blue kerchief her mother gave her into her bouquet. Diandra admired her appearance in the cheval mirror that stood in the corner. She shook her head slightly to jingle the diamond chandelier earrings Benét had leant her and wiggled her toe to feel the penny in her shoe. She could hear the sounds of Sadé and knew that the parents were being seated.

Seven would be at the altar awaiting her walk down the aisle.

Shaeyla entered the anteroom to see Diandra, a beautiful vision in her Sádéa original gown. The sweeping skirt rustled as she made her way across the room. She was surprised at the gown Diandra chose because the tight bodice gave way to a romantic skirt with a flirty flounce. The matching veil attached to the pink and white crystal tiara stopped at her waist.

"You look beautiful."

"Thanks. I feel beautiful."

Shaeyla felt her eyes misting. "Don't cry because I will and, well, you know-."

"I won't," Diandra said, grabbing a tissue from the side table to dab at her eyes. She was cautious not to ruin her makeup. She turned back to Shaeyla.

"Are you ready?"

"Yes."

"Okay. Let's get you married."

Shaeyla ushered the group into the vestibule, and prodded each one to ascend the aisle. On cue, Diandra placed her hand into the arm of her uncle and proudly made her way to Seven. She was careful to mark her strides determinedly, when in reality, she wanted to run into his arms.

Her uncle gave her away and placed her hand in Seven's. The couple had eyes for no one else as the musician sang *For You*. They cried as they exchanged vows and their tears mingled as the minister pronounced them man and wife.

The audience let out a loud cheer at the prolonged kiss.

"Man let her go!" someone yelled out, causing the crowd to laugh.

The receiving line was done quickly. Diandra was trying to rush through the guests, not realizing how many people she had invited. Next came an endless number of photographs that began to test the patience of the children. The photographer snapped the final shots and the bridal party headed towards the limos parked in front of the church. There was one for the bridesmaids and groomsmen and another for her and Seven.

Once inside the limo he wasted no time in drawing her into his arms to kiss her thoroughly. Uninterrupted he explored every crevice of her mouth. Starving for more. Her moans had him pressing her deeper into the seat of the car. He reached around trying to raise her dress up.

Reluctantly she tore away from him, "Baby, wait."

"What?" he asked raggedly between harsh breaths.

"We can't get busy in here. Much as I want to, we have the reception to get through. Then after that I am all yours. Open to *whatever* you heart desires."

"I knew I shouldn't have agreed to that 'wait until we're married' bull."

Rising away from her to get his body under control, the next four hours were going to test his patience and his will.

As she sat up and straightened her veil and reapplied her lipstick she leaned over to him.

"It's been hard on me as well. But I'm glad you did agree, because that will make tonight all the more special."

The head table faced the beautiful bank of windows that overlooked the harbor. The restaurant was aptly named *Windows* because of this view.

Shaeyla had done it again.

She created a beautiful indoor evening oasis under the stars. The pink and white theme for the wedding was a tribute to Diandra's mother who was a breast cancer survivor. The ceiling was adorned with a thousand sparkling pink and white lights. The tables were covered in white cloths with a pink overlay on which there was a striking centerpiece. Placed in an elongated tube vase were varying shades of pink and white long stemmed roses surrounded by baby's breath.

This brought the attention of the guest upward and allowed for them to converse with one another obstructing their views. The silver charger was the backdrop for the elegant dinner, salad, and dessert plates with a soft pink hue. The sterling silverware was tied in a white napkin with a pink bow engraved with 'Diandra and Seven' and the date of the wedding.

The whimsical placeholders, fashioned out of sterling silver like a three-tiered wedding cake, held the names of each guest and sat on a table near the entrance to the banquet hall.

The left side of the room held a lavish buffet of Maryland's best seafood: imperial blue crab, fish, oysters, and clams. Interspersed throughout were various salads placed on tiers in elaborate shell shaped servers. The ice sculptures reflected the lights in the ceiling and took pride of place at the appetizer station.

The wedding cake took first place in the dessert area as it sat in the center of six heart shaped cakes topped with fresh strawberries. The six-tiered confection was draped with edible pink and white roses. The butter cream icing held the one-of-a-kind cake topper of the black bride swept up into the grooms arms. Their accessories matched those of Seven and Diandra and were a gift from Shaeyla, who called in a favor from a client.

The smooth-jazz ensemble lent a feeling of mellowness to the affair. They would play for the first two hours while the band set up, then the band would play for the final two hours. Diandra had to have her go-go music.

The guest began to arrive in droves, and Shaeyla instructed two of the hostesses to help move the seating process along as the line began to increase.

She spotted Benét and Worthy walking towards the table where Kendra and Niall were seated as she placed the last hostess at the gift table. From her vantage point, she could see how Niall reacted to seeing Worthy and vice versa. Although they knew of each other and the importance they held in their circle, this was their first formal introduction.

• • • • •

Worthy saw the dark skinned man beside Kendra stand as they approached the table. He extended his hand, "You must be Worthy. I've heard a lot about you. It's good to finally meet you."

He held her hand in a firm handshake. Worthy eyed him then glanced down at Kendra and the love she saw there was enough for her.

"All I get is a handshake," she joked, moving around the table to give him a hug. "My girl is the happiest I've ever seen her. Welcome to the family."

With that completed they all hugged and kissed each other, teasing Shaeyla for being a romantic at heart and getting them the same shade of dress in different styles. Hers was a long gown with a halter neckline and a long slit exposing her creamy chocolate thigh while the empire waist of Kendra's dress hid her expanding middle.

The joy the women emanated, the joy they had in their friendship and lives showed in the smiles on their faces. Together they were striking. They were uniquely beautiful.

"I would love to stay and chat, but I have to get ready because they should be here shortly. Once the reception is in full swing, we are taking a group photo." Shaeyla said as she walked to the podium.

She reviewed her notes, enjoying the sounds of merriment around her. One thing she loved was a party and wedding receptions were the best, especially when it was her best friend getting married.

The tittering of the guests became louder and the signal from her assistant told her that the bridal party had arrived. Shaeyla moved closer to the microphone. It saved her from having to raise her voice while helping her gain the attention of the crowd.

"Ladies and gentlemen. Please take your seats. The bridal party has arrived."

She watched the guests scurry about; some to get appetizers while others went to the bar. *Nothing's changed. Black folk still killing themselves over free shit*, she thought, smiling to herself.

The limousines pulled into the entryway of the Renaissance Hotel in downtown Baltimore. Its magnificent stature stood gleaming in the twilight of the Inner Harbor.

Seven's nut-brown skin was flushed, his tie askew and his vest unbuttoned. Diandra's hand was on his crotch where his need for her strained against his zipper.

A discreet tap on the dividing window warned them before the driver lowered it slightly to announce their arrival at the hotel.

"Damn", he said before capturing her mouth beneath his.

Their breathing was heavy. The windows were steamed but thankfully the tint would hide that. Reluctantly he removed her hand, her attempts to ease his erection only making him harder.

Her tawny colored eyes were glassy. Her pupils dilated, giving evidence of their aroused states.

"Help me with the back of my dress."

Once presentable, Seven tapped on the door and the chauffeur opened it to assist Diandra and him from the car. The entire bridal party was waiting near the bank of elevators that would whisk them upstairs.

The group was laughing as the doors opened to the

restaurant level. Shaeyla was waiting to announce them to the guests. She lined them up according to the program before slipping back into the room. Seven and Diandra kissed until they heard their name called. As they entered the huge ballroom, the guests stood. He heard the familiar call of his fraternity from his brothers over the cheers of good will and laughter. Making their way to the head table, he saw the smiles of his family and friends and her girlfriends.

The pastor blessed the food once everyone was seated, and then the head table was served. The uniformed waiters moved swiftly and silently throughout the tables to ensure that each guest was served their entrée's timely and efficiently.

Shaeyla tapped on the microphone an hour later to ask for the best man and matron of honor to step forward to deliver their toasts.

With that completed, Seven and Diandra took their place in the center of the dance floor for their first dance. The sound of Pure Souls "We Must Be In Love" danced in the air as they swayed to the music. The sight of Seven singing the song to Diandra brought tears to her eyes. Seven cried too and this brought tears to the eyes of many, because the love was there for all to see.

Shaeyla kept the bridal party from dancing with them, because she knew that this song was special to the couple. She motioned for them to join the couple as Stevie Wonder's voice belted out "You and I". The bride moved to dance with her uncle and he with is mother, before they switched off and she danced with his father and he with her mother, after which the guests lined up for the apron dance with Diandra.

Seven made his way over to talk to Shaeyla to thank her for making the day beautiful.

"Hey", he gave her a friendly hug and kiss on her cheek. "You've outdone yourself again. This place looks magical-pink, but magical."

"I know. I'm amazed as well, because Diandra has never been into pink, but it was her wedding and she said this is what she always imagined it would look like."

"She could've wanted a wedding in a barn, so long as she married me."

"I know. Now go get your bride and you two walk around and mingle with your guests. I'll come and get you two in an hour or so to cut the cake."

She turned to advise the waiters to begin clearing the tables and preparing for the dessert. She also had them replenish the champagne as well as the coffee service area.

She advised the gift table attendants to begin loading the gifts into the trucks that would take them to the newlywed's new home. Shaeyla then told the hostess that she would be the caretaker of the envelope box, handing the contents over to Seven prior to their honeymoon departure.

Her attention was caught up by Benét's swift departure from the room. Wondering what happened to make her leave hurriedly, made her brow wrinkle in consternation, but her wondering was short lived as she spotted Kenny at the door with a ginger-hued honey on his arm.

Chapter 37- Benét's Embarrassment

The couple at the door stopped Benét in her tracks. There in the doorway stood Kenny and at his side was Isis.

Oh no he didn't bring another woman to her girls wedding! She screamed silently.

Benét had been thoroughly enjoying herself until that moment. She had to get out of there. She crossed the room to the double doors and made her way along the corridor to the ladies room. There she locked herself in a luxurious stall, unable to get the sight of them from her mind.

I can't believe he'd embarrass me like this! This final action made her realize that her marriage was over. She would've preferred being escorted, than come alone, but she had told Christian that she was going alone out of respect for Kenny. She had tried in vane earlier in the year to reconcile and get Kenny to talk to her, but he refused. She had thought about the situation constantly and believed that had the shoe been on the other foot she would've tried to work it out with him. Although it would've been a devastating blow to her marriage she believed that she loved him enough and had enough faith in their marriage to try to make it work.

Once she got over the hurt and pain at his stubbornness, the anger set in. That's what made seeing Christian all that more irresistible. Now she had nothing standing in the way of them hooking up. She didn't love him like she loved her husband, but he made the unbearable bearable and life fun. He had a great job and willingly wanted to step in and take up where Kenny left off.

Security was high on Benét's list of priorities; she liked not having to watch her spending. He too wanted her to stay home, but he was also talking children and she wasn't having that. Her kids were damn near grown and she didn't intend to start over.

Hell at first she was upset at losing the baby, but she knew it was a godsend. It was not meant for her to have had Christian's baby. She had been careless. Had she been paying attention to her body she would've noticed that she had missed her cycle. Instead she had been caught up. Her nose wide open for Christian, and her carelessness had her where she was today, on the brink of divorcing and messing with a younger man.

Christian claimed to be desperately in love with her, wanted to marry her, but she couldn't comprehend that. Her kids knew she was up to something because she had started staying out late. On the weekends they were with their father, she had taken to staying at Christians, advising them to call her on her cell.

She had to get herself together. As she splashed some water on her face the picture of Isis clinging to *her husband*! She caught the smug look in Kenny's face before leaving the room. She should've bought Christian with her. Reaching for her purse she pulled out her cell phone and called him. After several rings, his voice mail picked up. *Damn it Christian, where are you?* She paged him, refreshed her makeup and reentered the ballroom.

She stood in the doorway her eyes scanning the room for the sight of Kenny. She spotted him on the dance floor. Isis had her body pressed against his, her head on his chest. His hands seemed to be caressing her back slowly. She moved over to the buffet table closest to the dance floor. She had to see his face.

What is up with you, Benét? You're acting more like Shaeyla? It's been six months since your break up. You have to let him go.

Silently she castigated herself. Turning her back on them she fashioned her face in a cordial smile and before she lost her nerve she walked onto the floor straight for the swooning couple.

"Excuse me. May I cut in?"

"No, you may not," Kenny said perturbed at the interruption. He swung Isis away deeper into the throng of guests crowding the center of the dance floor.

Determinedly Benét followed stepping on toes and elbowing herself through the dancers until she found herself face-to-face with the couple.

She turned to Isis, "Listen, did Kenny tell you about us?"

"Yes he did."

"So then you know that he is married?"

"Actually separated."

"Whatever, listen, I don't want you in the middle of this."

"Chile please. What you don't want is for me to have him."

"Ladies we are not going to have this here. Benét, you need to recognize that it's over. I've moved on, and you should too. "

"But Kenny-." She reached out to him.

"No! By the end of the year-."

"By the end of the year, what, Kenny? What?"

"By the end of the year, our divorce will be final."

"You're so fucking smug. I am tired of apologizing to you. Begging you to listen to me and hear me out. Well I know this much is true, you won't have to worry about me bothering you anymore."

"Good, then maybe my *woman* and I can enjoy what's left of the reception in peace."

Slowly he turned away and resumed his dance. Inside he was riddled with emotion at seeing her face and hearing her voice.

"Kenny is you okay?" Isis asked.

Jerked back to the present he looked down into the woman in his arms and for a minute almost forgot her name.

"Yes, Isis I'm fine."

He didn't want to listen to her idle chatter. He placed a finger over her pursed lips.

"Shhh, let's put that scene out of our minds and enjoy the rest of the evening."

• • • • •

Benét watched Kenny walk away with Isis. She eyed the sly grin of triumph on the woman's face as Kenny led them to another corner of the dance floor.

Her hubris when it came to Kenny was enormous and this was a big blow to her ego. She just knew he wasn't going anywhere, regardless of their issues. It's her fault. Physically she was exhausted and emotionally drained yet she had to appear strong and unwavering when all she wanted to do was weep. Humiliated and disgusted she gazed around the room to find her girls. She needed them now. Needed their strength, wisdom, humor, sarcasm and wit to see her through the rest of the evening.

No what she needed was to call Christian and to tell him to bring his ass to the reception.

Chapter 38 - Here Comes Trouble

Shaeyla paled when she saw Christian walking through the doors of the reception hall.

"What in the hell is Benét trying to pull?" she asked herself.

Forcing back her shoulders she began to cross the room. Halfway there, Benét met her.

"What in the hell are you doing?" Shaeyla demanded of her friend.

"I am not going to let Kenny get the best of me today! He doesn't want me, well that's fine, but I refuse to be the side show circus in this act!"

Shaeyla not only heard the humiliation in her friend's voice, she saw a desperate need to save face in this situation.

"You know I hate scenes at my events Benét! Besides, how could you even contemplate this? *Of all days!* This is Diandra and Seven's *wedding day* and you and Kenny need to handle your childish attempts at one-upmanship some place else."

"Then we'll leave."

"No, unfortunately you can't. Not without Diandra wanting to know why. But stay away from Kenny and I will instruct him to do the same to you!"

Benét watched as Shaeyla turned away from her in a

huff. She knew she had messed up by inviting Christian, but at the time she didn't care.

Christian suddenly appeared before her. Dressed in a chocolate brown suit, shot through with tiny gold pin-stripes and contrasting tie, he looked extremely hand-some.

"I've been looking everywhere for you. I thought you were going to meet me at the door?" Christian said to Benét somewhat vexed.

Benét eyed him up and down. Showing with her eyes her satisfaction at seeing him and that she knew he was helpless against her direct brown stare.

Christian was powerless against her eyes. He had al-ways been. She knew it then, just like she knew it now. His anger at being left to wander the room dissipated. Even the awkwardness of the brief eye contact he made with her husband left him.

Benét embraced Christian. Pressing her tight curves into his body, she reached up to place a hot kiss on his lips. Slowly his tongue left his mouth and slid oh so slowly into hers. She heard his sigh of pleasure and began to feel his body harden. He reached up and pulled her arms away from his neck.

"You are pushing me to my limit," he said as he rested his head on hers.

She smiled wickedly, "That's the point."

She turned, taking his hand in hers, leading him to her table. She watched as her girl's eyes widened in surprise.

Diandra and Seven were making their way through

the throng of guests, happily talking and mingling with all their family and friends. She saw Diandra look at her and knew that she would get an earful once she returned from her honeymoon, but she would deal with that when the time came. For now, she had to show Kenny that he wasn't the only one who had someone who wanted her.

Benét introduced Christian to her friends. Shaeyla came over to the table to advise them that it was time for one last photo before the throwing of the bouquet and garter. After that they would cut the cake.

As Benét took her place in line with her girls, her eyes scanned the crowd for Kenny. She spotted him in an intimate conversation with Isis. It was then that she knew she had to try one last time to get him back.

He's just trying to make you jealous, she told herself. *Well, it worked.*

Not even Christian could stem the feeling of desolation she felt. She wanted her husband and family back and she wanted it soon.

♦ ♦ ♦ ♦ ♦

Kendra touched a hand to her stomach. For the second time in minutes, she felt a cramp in her abdomen. She leaned over and whispered to Niall that she had to use the ladies room, but the worried expression on her face alerted him.

"Kendra, what's wrong. Is everything okay?"

"I don't know, but I am feeling crampy and I don't want to take any chances."

"Let's go. I'm taking you to the hospital."

Kendra instantly shook her head. "No, that would cause too many questions. Besides I don't want to ruin the rest of the evening."

"I don't give a damn about ruining anything," Niall told her as he stood and helped her to her feet.

He turned to find Shaeyla walking towards them.

"Kendra isn't feeling well, so we are going to head out. Can you say our goodbyes?" Niall said, not waiting for a response.

Hurriedly he walked out of the reception hall to enter the elevator. He watched Kendra as she flinched in pain.

"Another cramp?" he asked, willing the elevator would move faster.

"Yes." she said as a tear slid from her eye. "Niall I am scared."

He pulled her securely into his arms. As the doors opened, reaching into his pocket he pulled out his valet slip. Minutes later the car pulled up and he lifted Kendra into his arms and gently placed her in the truck. She was now openly crying and his heart was beating strongly in his chest. He was afraid but couldn't show her. He had to be strong.

He pulled out of the parking area and into the light evening traffic. He raced across town to the Harris General Hospital, sliding into the emergency room bay. He lifted her from the car and rushed inside. "My wife is pregnant and she is cramping, I need your help," Niall yelled frantically.

The nurse on duty came around the desk and instructed an orderly to place her in a chair and into an empty room.

Niall walked over to the appointed chair and pulled out his cell phone to contact Shaeyla. He did not tell them that they were going to the doctors, he'd told them they were heading home. Besides, Kendra did not want to ruin Diandra and Seven's day.

"Shaeyla Andrews"

"Shaeyla, Niall here."

"Hey Niall, what's up?"

"Listen I didn't want to alarm you, but I bought Kendra to the hospital. She was--" Shaeyla cut him off.

"The hospital! What! Why didn't you say that was where you were going when you left?"

"Because she didn't want to ruin Diandra's day. Listen, she was cramping, and the doctor is in with her now. I don't know if she told you or not, but we had a scare a couple of months ago and the doctor put her on bed rest."

"Damn Niall! You should've told us."

"She didn't want you, any of you to worry."

Shaeyla swore under her breath, "How did we miss that?"

"I won't mention this to Diandra. She has had a trying time today as it is. I will tell Benét, and if you're still there by the time we leave, we'll meet you at the hospital."

"Look Shaeyla, I appreciate that, but I'm here for her now…so there is no need for you to come down."

Shaeyla was silent for a moment. She didn't want to hurt Niall, but if her girl was in distress, they were going to be there.

"Okay, Niall, I understand."

As Niall hung up his phone, he wondered how long it would take them to wrap things up. He knew that nothing would keep them away -- he shouldn't have even tried.

♦ ♦ ♦ ♦ ♦

Shaeyla hung up her phone and immediately went in search for Benét. She spotted her cuddling up to Christian.

"Excuse us for a moment, please," she said to Christian as she drew Benét away from the table.

"What's wrong?"

Shaeyla went outside into the hallway. "Niall just called, he had to take Kendra to the hospital."

"What!" Benét exclaimed.

"Calm down, she was cramping or something. Anyway I told him to keep us informed."

"Fuck that 'keep us informed shit.'" We need to go there now." Benét said.

On re-entering the room to gather their belongings, the ladies paused as they heard an unfamiliar voice over the microphone.

A s the women reentered the reception, their eyes flew to the man on the microphone. His face was vaguely familiar. However, Shaeyla, appalled that this person dared to interrupt her well-planned reception.

She broke away from her friends, intent on removing the microphone from him when she noticed the looks that Diandra and Seven exchanged between each other.

Diandra was a pale shade of beige. Her skin had gone completely ashen as she turned to Shaeyla and mouthed 'Mason'...

Shaeyla touched a hand to her forehead. Everything made sense now. The tittering and laughing she overheard in the church. The way in which the women from the salon stopped talking whenever she came near. Mason was the person they were talking about. The phrase she'd overhead was "he gave up his shorties"; at the time it meant nothing to Shaeyla, but now the pieces were falling into place.

Something had happened between her girl and Mason, and it was recent enough to cause a talk amongst her employees at her wedding.

Diandra rushed to the front of the room. The blood was pounding in her temples.

Seven stood staring at her, embarrassed as she ran to

Mason's side. His breath quickened and he was humiliatingly conscious of the scrutiny he was receiving from their guest.

"I told you girl. I told you not to marry ole boy! But no! You didn't listen! You tried to carry me and play me. Naw, shortie, I ain't the one to be fucked with like that," Mason's voice boomed throughout the room.

"Mason. I told you that I was in love with Seven."

"Is that right? You didn't say that the other night, when you were riding my dick."

The crowd gasped.

Seven's embarrassment turned to fury.

"Diandra!" he yelled. "What is going on?"

Diandra turned, her hands wrenching together feverishly. She didn't want to have this conversation here. Not here on her wedding day. Got dammit! Mason was ruining it for her. She knew it. She felt all day that something ominous was going to happen, but as the day wore on and nothing happened, she let her guard down. And this is the result. Her marriage was over before it even began.

Seven advanced on the two people at the podium. He wanted to tear Mason apart. He wanted *his wife* to answer him. He stopped in front of her.

"Diandra. Look at me."

Diandra raised her head. She swallowed the despair in her throat. Her expression was one of mute wretchedness.

Seven's face was a glowering mask of rage. "I asked you a question. What does he mean about the other night?" A sudden thin chill hung on the edge of his words.

"Seven...I didn't want you to find out like this," she replied in a low, tormented voice.

"Find out about what," he roared.

She flinched at the tone of his voice, "F-f-f-find out about Mason and me."

She reached out to touch him.

He flung her hand off him. He couldn't bear the sight of her, let alone her touch. Today was supposed to be the best day of his life. He awoke this morning feeling euphoric. He was marrying the woman of his dreams. The day was picture book perfect. And then this happens. As he looked around the room his eyes rested on the anguished faces of his parents.

His mother stood up. "I told you not to marry this tramp!" she flung at Diandra.

"What a minute, bitch." Diandra's mother stood up. "My daughter is not a tramp."

"Oh really? So I guess sleeping with this man before marrying my son is okay with you?" Seven's mother asked.

"Hell no! I ain't saying she was right. But I be damned if I'll let you call my daughter out of her name!"

Seven silently signaled to his father to escort his mother from the premises. Slowly, his family began to exit the building, grumbling loudly.

Diandra's family followed along with the rest of the guests.

Remaining in the room were the bridal party, the wait staff, the musicians, and Shaeyla, Benét, and Worthy.

Shaeyla and the girls were speechless. They didn't know what to say. Shaeyla's mind was on overdrive. She could only handle one crisis at a time. But today, she had issues with Benét and her love triangle, Kendra and the baby, and now this shit. She walked to the wait staff and musicians, asking them to leave.

The women huddled together whispering.

"What the fuck did she do?" Benét asked. "Dammit, didn't she learn from the mistake I made?"

"Obviously not," Worthy said derisively.

"I can't take this. This is just some extra shit I refuse to deal with now," Shaeyla said.

Worthy and Benét looked at her. They knew that Shaeyla would break in a time of crisis, and she was on her way. Although the wedding wasn't hers per se...this day was her baby. She reveled in creating memorable moments and events that people talked about for days.

Not only would they talk about this they would associate the chaos and confusion that followed with Events To Remember.

Seven had never been one to hit a woman but Mason's words had him ready to two-piece Diandra. A white-hot rage took over him and in two steps he was near her. He gripped her upper arm and dragged her into the reception hall's small anteroom where less than an hour before he had sat with his bride professing their love for each other.

He flung her away from him and she fell backwards against the wall. His broad shoulders heaved his expression grim as he eyed her.

Diandra's mouth opened in dismay. No words seemed appropriate, "I'm sorry," was all she could utter.

Eyes blazing with anger, "Yes, you are sorry," Seven said in a matter of fact voice.

Seven spoke his voice hard and ruthless. "It's just like they say, black women don't know what they want. You think I didn't see the little game Benét & Kenny played today? I overlooked it because *I* was so *happy*. You were finally mine. MINE!"

Diandra fell to the floor. She pulled her knees to her chest, resting her arms to hide her face. She was beyond tears. Seven was right. She and her friends were selfish and stupid. Outside of Kendra, they all seemed to be stuck on stupid when it came to their relationships with men.

She sat there mired in her own misery as Seven continued to castigate her.

"For six years I watched how men used and abused you. For six years, I bided my time, waiting for you to see me. Notice me. Yet you continued to want the thugs and just when I thought I had you, you pull a fucked up move like this."

There was a long brittle silence. "Well today ain't your happily ever after. I am so disgusted with you and your whorish, trifling ass ways, that as much as I love you..."

Diandra's head jerked up when she heard him speak of his love for her.

Seven saw the realization dawn in her eyes.

"Yes, I love you, but baby, sometimes love ain't enough. I got to let you go. You are obviously not the woman that I thought you were, and because of that I am not the man for you."

His words penetrated her fogged brain. "Seven, what are you saying?"

His eyes raked her from head to toe. "I'm saying; I don't want you. Go run after that punk ass nigga you gave my pussy to last night...'cause I'm done. You can stay here if you want, I'm up out of here."

Diandra struggled to her feet. "B-b-but what am I supposed to tell people," she asked in a hushed and anguished voice.

"I don't give a fuck what you tell them," Seven scoffed. "Do you need to tell them anything? I mean your nigga said it all now didn't he?" He turned and made his way to the door.

"But… what about the house?"

Her question stopped him, he turned, and his cold black eyes impaled her.

"What about it. You're name was never on the deed, so technically it's my house. So you need to make living arrangements and have someone come move your shit."

Diandra's stomach clinched tight with fear. Seven leaving was a litany that played in her mind stabbing at her heart. She watched as he opened the door and left. Never once did he turn back. She had finally gotten what she wanted and fucked it up. She dropped her head to her chest and rocked back and forth, the pain deep, and hot scalding tears burned her cheeks.

• • • • •

Shaeyla watched as Seven strode to her, a look of disappointment on his face. He placed an arm around her shoulder, "we need to talk," was all he uttered.

Shaeyla let herself walk with him although she was concerned; she kept her facial expression neutral. There was more than enough talk about this day already. *What the fuck is it now* she wondered.

In the hallway he turned to her.

"I need you to return all the gifts and move Diandra's stuff from my house."

"What? Seven, what is going on?"

Seven turned his head toward the ceiling before looking back at her.

"Look don't play dumb with me. You know damn well what is going on. Your girl fucked up, I told her to kick rocks, and that is it. You know I can't stay married to her after this. Besides the fact of the complete humiliation and embarrassment I felt, she fucked another man...not a few months ago. But last fucking night!"

Shaeyla heard his anger in his voice. His entire body screamed out pissed off.

"Seven, y'all love each other. I know she fucked up, but can't you work through this," she asked as a last ditch effort to help her friend.

"No Shaeyla. I can't. Just-," his voice trailed off and he threw his hands up and walked away.

The increasing buzz from the on lookers had Shaeyla slapping on her poker face. She smiled and walked back into the reception hall. Unfortunately, this was going to be the talk of the town. Already folks were on their cell phones with the "hot gossip" for the day.

Her eyes scanned the crowd for Worthy and Benét. She saw them walking towards the same door Seven had just come through and she picked up the pace to join them.

"What the fuck is going on," Benét asked as she reached them.

Sighing deeply, "It's a mess," she said.

They opened the door to find Diandra on the floor. She looked up to see who it was, and cried harder.

"He left me," she gasped out, "he left me."

Benét placed her hands on her hips, "What the fuck did you expect?"

"Benét," Shaeyla scolded.

"No Shaeyla, she needs to hear this. Didn't she learn from my mistake? It wasn't like you fucked the nigga last month. It was the night before your *wedding*." Benét stopped to catch her breath.

"What the hell were you thinking," she asked shaking her head.

Diandra shook her head. The tears slowly subsiding.

"I know I fucked up."

"Yeah, you did. And with a good brother too. I knew your ghetto ass didn't deserve him," Benét stated.

"Fuck you!" Diandra yelled. "You got room to talk. Your marriage is fucked up too and at least I didn't get pregnant."

Benét paused for a minute.

"Oh that was low, but you know what? I am paying for it everyday. And now you're gonna know how it feels."

Shaeyla jumped in to stop the bickering.

"Look, Seven came up to me and asked me to return the gifts and to move your stuff out of his house."

Diandra look cross-eyed, "He what?"

"You heard me," Shaeyla said.

She continued, "He told me he was done with you. You can stay with me until you get yourself sorted out. But for right now you need to heed his words."

Worthy spoke up from the corner of the room. "We always fuck up our relationships. We get ourselves in jacked up situations and then not want to suffer the consequences and repercussions of our actions."

Worthy stopped and let her eyes rest on each of her friends.

"The sad thing is, we condone each others bullshit. You and Benét had good men and you allowed dick to fuck it up. There are a million sisters that would die to have either of the men y'all had," Worthy intoned, shrugging her shoulders at the craziness of it all.

"In my case, I allowed drugs to mess me up. Allowed it to take me over and ruin my life. It got my child taken away from me. I mean I fucked up royally and each day I have to try to live without drugs. In Shaeyla's case, she has a desire to be loved; yet she hasn't even chosen the right men. The only one of us that seems to have gotten it right is Kendra."

Worthy leaned back against the wall. She didn't know where her sudden knowledge came from but she wanted her words to marinate in her friend's minds because what she said was long overdue.

Niall paced back and forth as he waited for news from the doctor. He couldn't keep going through this. Hell, the baby wasn't here and he was becoming more familiar with this facility than he wanted to. He looked at his watch for the fifth time in as many minutes, shaking his head, praying that Kendra and the baby were okay.

But if she wasn't, if complications would arise and it came down to the baby or Kendra, the baby would be sacrificed. He thought that two months ago when they came here the last time and the feeling was even stronger now. He loved Kendra too much to live without her. They could always have another baby and if not they could and would adopt, but he couldn't see himself marrying nor fathering a child with any other woman but Kendra.

The waiting room doors swooshed open and he turned to see Dr. Peoples walking towards him.

"Doc, is everything okay. How is Kendra?"

"Mr. Adams, calm down everything is fine."

"The cramping. I thought that was fixed the last time."

"Well I have placed your fiancée on complete bed rest. She is only to get out of bed for bathroom breaks and that is it. If she follows my instructions, there is no reason why her last few months, although boring, should be without incident."

"Don't worry, I will make sure that happens. I can work from home to keep an eye on her. Can I see her now?"

"Yes."

Niall walked into the room they had placed Kendra in. She was sleeping with both hands resting on her stomach. Absently she rubbed her swollen middle, as if to sooth herself and their unborn child.

He loved the two of them so much, that looking at this picture he would've been hard pressed to make a snap decision about whom to save. He wanted them both in his life. As he stepped farther into the room, he slid into the chair beside the bed and placed his hand over hers.

She opened her eyes to look at him. Tears still glistened on her lashes.

"Niall, I am so sorry."

"Shh...there is nothing for you to be sorry about. The doctor explained to me that this happens sometimes. She is placing you on complete bed rest and I am going to work from home until we deliver our little one."

His hand squeezed hers in a reassuring grip.

"What about my job?"

"Well, you can work from home also, although I am going to limit you to a few hours a day. And your associates can pick up the rest of the slack. I'll even stop in periodically to make sure everything is running smoothly."

"The girls... I have to call-"

"I've talked to Shaeyla and she is informing Benét and Worthy, but not Diandra because we all know she would cancel her honeymoon," placing a finger over her mouth, to quiet her.

"I don't want to ruin their day," she cried on a hiccup.

"You haven't. She will be upset, but she will get over it. I've asked them to let me have this time with you, but if I know your girls they are probably en route."

Kendra shook her head. "No they will be worried, but they won't come tonight, because of Diandra." Kendra knew that with a certainty.

Just as she said that, she heard Niall's cell phone bleeping. She smiled. "I bet that's one of them right now."

Niall opened his phone and handed it to her.

"Hello," said Kendra.

"Kendra, are you okay? What did the doctor say?" She was never great in a crisis. Her questions came like rapid fire, one after the other.

Niall could hear the questions and he took the phone from Kendra.

"Shaeyla, the doctor placed her on complete bed rest until she delivers."

"Oh, okay. So we need to work up a schedule so that she is never alone during the day while you're at work."

"Thanks, but I'm going to work from home. I am going to take care of her."

His statement was met with silence. Shaeyla wanted to protest, but knew she had to concede. It wouldn't be easy to let go and have a stranger doing what they used to do, but Niall wasn't a stranger, he was going to be their brother, family.

"Okay, no problem," said Shaeyla. "But if you ever for any reason need to go out, call one of us and we will be there."

"We are here for you too. You're part of our family now."

Niall smiled, and thanked her. Those women stuck together no matter what the problem.

The ride from the hospital to the rehab center to drop off Worthy was done in silence. It was unspoken but they were all worried about Kendra, sending up silent prayers that everything would be okay. They wanted this baby so much and they could see how it had bought them closer together, if anything should happen they honestly didn't think their relationship would survive.

Worthy broke the silence.

"I hope and pray that everything is okay?"

"Yeah, so do I." Shaeyla said.

"Me too," chimed Benét.

Worthy shook her head. "I never thought I would say this, but I'm glad that I won't be around when y'all tell Diandra what happened."

They laughed. "I'm not arguing about this," said Shaeyla. "We did what needed to be done. There was no need for her to find out about this tonight."

Benét shook her head in agreement.

"Besides, if she was here, she'd be knee deep worrying me about the decorations and you know Seven hired me to surprise Diandra."

"He loves her so much," Worthy said on a sigh.

"Yes. I had someone that used to love me like that too." Benét said despairingly.

Shaeyla sighed. "Since you bought it up, what was up with having Christian at the reception today?"

Worthy looked at Benét. She was just as shocked as the rest of them to see him walk into the room, but they understood why she did it.

"I know why he was there," Worthy said in Benét's defense, "and so do you Shaeyla. Hell she was saving face. You saw Kenny come in with that other chick. I'd have done the same thing."

"I'm not denying that I wouldn't have done the same thing!" Shaeyla shouted, "I'm questioning why today?"

Benét reared her head back in defiance at Shaeyla's tone of voice.

"Why the hell do you think? You of all people should know how it feels to see the one you love with another."

That crack stopped the tirade exploding from Shaeyla. Benét was right but it was the principle of it all.

"You're right. I'm just saying it's the principle of it all."

Worthy could tell that this could easily escalate into something so much more.

"Listen, let's drop this and to be sure, Shaeyla, drop off Benét then take me to the clinic."

"No, you'll miss curfew if I do that."

"Not if you ball I won't."

Shaeyla looked at Benét to see how she felt about it.

"I'm cool with that," Benét stated.

When the words left her mouth Shaeyla gunned the engine and headed for Benét's.

Thirty minutes later, she pulled into the rehab center

parking area with minutes to spare. They stepped out of the car and walked arm-in-arm to the building.

Worthy turned to her, "Thanks so much. Despite everything that happened today, I still enjoyed being with you all."

Shaeyla laughed, "I know the drama was just like old times."

Worthy smiled, "True. True. And I miss it so much."

Shaeyla could see the tears welling in her friend's eyes. "Don't start that, because if you do I won't stop."

Worthy sucked up her sorrow and turned to step into the building. She watched as Shaeyla walked back to her vehicle and drove off. She didn't turn away until she saw the tail lights disappear.

The first person she ran into was Bliss. She was standing in the entryway to the break room. *She always snuck around.* Worthy thought.

"Have a nice time?" Bliss asked.

"As a matter of fact I did," Worthy said.

She was cool with Bliss and all, but she didn't intend to go into detail. Sisters in this place were jealous. Although Bliss had been out of sight she had seen the looks of envy on their faces earlier when her girls had picked her up.

Bliss walked over and fingered the fine material of her dress. She noted the matching purse and shoes.

"Your girls really went all out for you. This outfit must've cost a mint."

"That's what girlfriends, true sister girlfriends do Bliss. We take care of one another in good times and bad."

"Whatever, man," Bliss scoffed as she crossed the room and headed for the stairs.

Worthy watched her, and then followed her up to their room. From the first day she met Bliss she had this gut feeling about her, but she couldn't quite put her finger on it. *I know her from somewhere though,* she said to herself. There was something about her that Worthy couldn't say she didn't like, but didn't trust. That's it. She didn't really trust Bliss but in a place like this, she had to trust someone. You had to buddy up to make it through the program, its unfortunate for her that she was paired with Bliss.

As she walked into the room and undressed, she placed her dress, shoes, and purse back in the garment bag Kendra had delivered it in. She then turned and placed it into her locker, turned off her bedside lamp and was asleep when her head hit the pillow.

• • • • •

Bliss watched Worthy as she did her nightly routine. She had spoken to JJ earlier in the day and told him about her fancy ass wedding. She had gotten upset when JJ asked how she looked. He'd told her that before he had gotten Worthy strung out, she used to be as fine as her loud mouth ass girlfriends. That Bliss didn't want to hear, but JJ was her man and what he said goes. She never argued with him. He asked and she obeyed it was that simple. Her face turned into a nasty scowl that is all Worthy had to do, but no she had to fuck up and get her man locked up. But that doesn't last; he was going to be out soon around the time her and Worthy were released from rehab. She didn't give a fuck about Worthy or her girlfriends. JJ had told her to make sure Worthy didn't stay sober once she was released and that was what she was going to do. She just had to get a good plan.

The next day, at Carembe Books and Coffee House, Benét and Kenny sat eyeing each other as if they were strangers. Benét had never felt so lost and empty as she did today. How was she supposed to combat her anger at seeing him with Isis? Did she even have a right to be upset or mad after what she had put him through? She was the one responsible for the breakup of her marriage. She had turned their happy home into the battlefield that it had been before Kenny leaving. She continued to look at him as his eyes held nothing for her. She would've been able to deal with his contempt, but his bored put on air was devastating to her ego. *No one treats me this way,* her mind screamed. Yet, she knew she had to hold on to her self-control and not demand that her husband thinks about what he was doing.

He broke into her thoughts. "Well are you going to stare at me all day? Or does this meeting have a purpose?"

Shakily she stated, "I think we need to talk about our situation, Kenny."

"What about it?"

"For starters, when did you start seeing Isis?"

He shook his head in disbelief. "You know what Benét, your ego never ceases to amaze me. What gives you the right to ask me about who I'm seeing?

"I'm still your wife," she stated.

"Ha, funny how you didn't remember that while you were fucking Kane! Bit-! Woman you have lost your mind bringing me out here to question me..." he stopped. "When did you start seeing Kane?"

Benét was taken aback by his vehement response. Yes, she was wrong for asking but she had to know if there was still a chance for her marriage to work. Besides the love she felt for him, she needed his financial security. She loved knowing that her bills were paid and her material needs met. Her girls teased her about it all the time, but it was the truth. Security in a relationship was high on her list. It was one of the deciding factors in marrying Kenny. She hadn't been in love with him when they initially married, but she had learned to love him. She had learned to enjoy his company and his loving.

"Listen Kenny," she said, her voice shaky with emotion. "I know that I fucked up, okay? I know that I am the cause for your moving out. For the break up of our marriage, but I need to know if we can work this out? If it's Christian you're worried about, I can tell you that I will stop seeing him. I promise if you take me back, that I'll never do this again."

Kenny sat in silence through her diatribe. His eyes drank from the sight of her. He loved her so much, but he couldn't trust her and trust was everything to him. At that moment, he knew that their marriage was over. Regardless of how much he was hurting and wanted to make her hurt, he knew that he couldn't live with her without questioning her every move and second-guessing her every word, thought, or deed. That was too much like being a bitch to him, so he had made up his mind to remove himself from her. Remove him from the heartache and pain that she had caused him.

Kane was only part of their problem. The other part had been his impotence.

"No Benét, there is no saving our marriage because *my* marriage must have trust. And the fact of the matter is I don't trust you. God knows with all my heart, body, and soul, I still love you, but without the trust; we have nothing."

He placed a bill on the table to cover their drinks and proceeded to leave.

"Kenny, wait."

He stopped where he stood, his back still facing her.

"I'm sorry for all the hurt and pain I caused you."

"I'm sorry too," he said and walked out the door.

She watched as he walked away from her for the last time. Grabbing her purse, she walked teary-eyed to her car where she sat hunched over the steering wheel, crying for the loss of her former life.

• • • • •

Across the parking lot, Kenny sat in his truck, watching as Benét walked to her car. A silent tear slipped down his cheek. He wanted to tell her that everything would be okay and that they could be together again, but his mind saw her making love to Kane. His body felt the anguish of the doctor's words that fateful day in the hospital *"I'm sorry but we lost the baby."*

Each time he thought of that it hit him that she had betrayed him and their marriage in the worst way. But to find out that she had betrayed him with his protégé was a double kick. He always wondered when their affair had started. Was it the day he introduced her to him at home or was it on the campus of Harris State College? His mind still held questions but he promised himself he would never ask her. He didn't want to know. It was bad enough that after almost a year from the incident and several months of separation, his mind still painted a very vivid picture of his wife in the throes of passion.

The beeping of his cell phone stopped his thoughts. Reaching into his pocket, he glanced down to see Isis calling. *Isis.* What was he going to do with her?

He saw Benét put her car in gear and pull out of her space. Mindlessly, he turned his phone off, shutting out thoughts of Isis. He started his truck and headed back to his spot. His new living quarters did not feel like his home. Initially it was a place for him to heal and grieve for his marriage. However as time moved on, he had come to realize that it would be his space for a few years or more. In his mind, other than his children, he could not imagine sharing his living area with anyone but his wife. *You are crazy to let her out of your life.* He loved her. He craved her touch, voice, and laughter. *So why are you letting her go? With love comes forgiveness. With love comes trust... and she took that the moment she moved into the arms of another man.* Kenny's tumultuous thoughts made him angry. He was dating Isis now. He needed to concentrate on that he told himself as he paced across the floor.

No she wasn't Benét and never would be, but she was frank, open, and honest about what she wanted. She wasn't duplicitous and if she was, who cared really? They were just dating--there was no expression of monogamy on their part. She could and probably did whatever she wanted to do.

Isis was just something to do. Someone for him to kill time with. She was fun, and very different from Benét, but he would never love her, and he damn sure wasn't trying to put her on lock. Not when he still loved his wife. His heart slammed against his chest...*he still loved his wife!* He had a lot of thinking to do. He knew how much it cost Benét to come to him and pour her heart out like that. He shook his head. He couldn't give into her. He wanted to so badly, he wanted their life back the way it used to be, but it had to be on his terms. On his time, and only when he was ready. With that thought in mind he exited his truck and entered his home.

Kendra lay in the bed, utterly defeated. Her will had virtually disappeared since the tragic stillbirth of her baby. Instinctively her hands moved over her now flat stomach. Her face was drawn and gaunt, a pale shell of her former self. Burying her head in the pillow to avoid conversation with Niall she feigned sleep. *I am so tired of him hovering over me.*

Niall stopped in the doorway. She had barely spoken to him or anyone for months. He was exasperated trying to convince her and show her that he loved her. Her weight had dropped dramatically. She ate very little of nothing, claiming she wasn't hungry. She even refused to eat for her girls who invaded his home from the moment their precious son had passed and every day since.

The ladies were a nuisance in the beginning. Each of them had an opinion, especially Benét who claimed to know so much about postpartum depression because she was the only one friend to have given birth. He got tired of coming home to his house to one or all of them. He knew they meant well, but hell, he was supposed to be the one to care for her. It was his job to make sure that she had everything, his job to provide for her in good times and bad. Her mumbling stopped him.

"What?"

She didn't know she had spoken the words aloud until then.

"Baby." Niall hedged closer to the bed before gingerly sitting down. For the past month this was her sanctuary. She had set up her room in the nursery they had enjoyed decorating together for the life they had created.

Swinging out from the covers she screamed at him in frustration. "I said I am tired of you fucking hovering over me! Shit! Leave me alone."

"Kendra!"

She jumped from the bed and grabbed her jeans from the floor. She threw on the same T-shirt she had on yesterday and walked towards the door.

"What a minute!" Gripping her arm he swung her around to face him. Her eyes looked dead, like she didn't even see him, her struggles that of a stranger.

"Let me go!"

"No! I am tired of this shit Kendra! You think you're the only one hurt by this? Do you?"

"You don't hurt like I do."

"What! Are you even listening to yourself? What the hell do you mean I don't hurt like you? I lost my son too!"

"I lost more. I carried him for nine months. Nine months of feeling him move within me. Nine months of watching my body grow and feel the changes of that happening. No, Niall, you don't *know* what its like."

She tried to turn away from, but he pulled her back to him, clasping his arms around her middle.

"No Kendra, calm down," he whispered harshly.

She was hysterical. He felt her body trembling before huge sobs racked her body. Her legs gave way and he scooped her up into his arms, moved out of the room and into the master suite.

"No, I want to go back to the nursery," she said, her attempts at getting him to release her futile.

"No. From now on you're going to sleep here with me. I am calling the doctor in the morning and we are going to grief counseling with other couples."

Her body stiffened in shock. "Th-ther-therapy?" she hiccupped.

"Yes. Kendra. I love you but I *need* you too. I need you to help comfort me also."

She looked at him in confusion.

"Yes. I lost the baby, but on top of that *I lost you*. You totally withdrew from me, leaving me alone to grieve. For the past month I have been holding on to my emotions around you. I have been coming into the room in the middle of the night holding and soothing your grief stricken body."

Disoriented she looked at him.

"Niall...". She saw the tears falling from his eyes. She heard the distress in his voice as the dam broke and he succumbed to his grief.

Her lower lip trembled. Her emptiness, the confusion and loneliness meshed together in a wave of yearning. Yearning to heal her broken heart and mend his grief. Watching Niall's tall stature shrink before her eyes brought her back to her senses. *What was she doing? How could she forget this man? This man who loved her from the beginning.* Sliding down to the floor she opened her arms to comfort him.

Together they held each other emptying their souls through tears. They cleansed their broken hearts as they soothed each other's pain over the loss of their son and the loss of their own intimacy.

Kendra felt doubly sad as she didn't even realize that she had pulled away from Niall, yet she had. She hadn't believed he could hurt as much as she did because he didn't carry their son, but as she looked back, she saw how ludicrous that belief was. Together with their love they had created a new life, a life which God had a better plan for, and in her selfishness she withdrew into herself because she was mad. Mad at God for taking away her happiness. Mad at God for taking the one thing she desired and loved more than anything and that was the fear of losing her man. She still couldn't believe in her mind that Niall loved her for her. Although he had shown her unconditional love and support over the past year, she still had her doubts. And she had let those doubts cloud her judgment and poison her mind, body, and soul against the father of her child. The true love of her life.

Lifting her hands to his face, she used her thumbs to wipe the tears from his eyes. It was her turn to comfort him, and to tell him how sorry she was.

With sobs still racking her now slender frame, she began a litany of words.

"I'm sorry", she said repeatedly. "I love you and I'm sorry."

Niall shook his head. His voice at first wobbly became strong as he lifted them from the floor. "I'm sorry too and I love you so much."

Pulling her down to the bed, he turned her away from him and wrapped his body around hers. He didn't want to make love; he just basked in the feel of her pressed up against his body again. He had his woman back and he was never letting her go again. He heard her sigh, and felt her pulse relax as she drifted off into her first restful sleep since---well since their loss. Kissing the top of her head, he squeezed her tight, and then he closed his eyes before he too drifted off to sleep.

Shaeyla sat on her deck thinking about the direction in which she needed to take her life. After watching the love continue to blossom between Diandra and Seven, she knew that it was decision time.

I have to stop seeing Mitchell. For the past few months, I could feel the change in our relationship; yet again I didn't want to face the reality that it was over. Surprisingly enough I feel much stronger. I don't need him any more than I needed Randy. I wanted him. I liked togetherness, but not being tolerated. If I'm honest with myself I'll admit that Benét was right again. She told me last year that I didn't love him, instead she told me I became fixated on an ideal and went with it. Her words were, "Honestly girl, I don't know where you get the gene of hanging onto to shit that isn't working." She was right. Just like my relationship with Randy, I hung onto something that wasn't working. Mitchell will never give me the type of relationship that I desire. Talk about a glutton for punishment. Now here I am again doing the same thing, but the difference this time is that I know that it's over. I won't shed any tears because this is a bittersweet realization.

Then there is Solomon. He doesn't know it, but he has found the love of his life and its time for me to tell him that. Besides, they began as friends. Yes, the chemistry was there, but in the back of my mind I somehow knew that we wouldn't work. That's when it hit her. *I am going to call them for a meeting and tell them both exactly what it is I'm feeling. Kill two birds with one stone.* Life is too short for me and for them to hold onto a love unworthy.

After placing a phone call to their assistants she called Benét, who picked up on the first ring.

"Hello."

"Hey girl, how are you?"

"I'm fine. How are you?"

"I have been sitting here thinking and I am going to tell Mitchell that I cannot see him anymore." This statement was met with silence.

"Benét?"

"I heard you. Hey, I say it's about damn time! His shelf life would've been up for me a long time ago, but your ass..."

"Yes, I know. I know I have a hard time letting things go. I was just thinking about Kendra losing the baby, and Diandra and Seven splitting up. I also thought about your situation and all that combined made me ask myself what I want. Why do I have this man in my life that obviously is out for self?"

"And?"

"And, I called his assistant to set up a meeting tomorrow to tell him. On his turf that it's over."

"Awww shit yeah! I wish I could be a fly on the wall," Benét cheered. She was so glad her girl had wised up. Hell she thought she would've been a better judge of character after breaking up with Randy. But she knew how Shaeyla thought and she thought that Mitchell Steele was the type of man she needed when what she needed was a man that would treat her special. Neither Mitchell nor Solomon was the one. Benét had to admit that Solomon surprised her because he didn't seem like the type to be so indecisive.

"Okay, now that you're taking care of Mitch, what are you going to do about Solomon?"

"You're not going to believe this but I called to set up the meeting with both of them. I figured why not kill two birds with one stone?"

"Have you thought about how this could affect your company?"

"Yes, I have, and I'm prepared to lose their business if it comes to that. I'm counting on them being businessmen though, but you know men, we'll have to see."

"Well, all I can say is it sounds like I have my girl back and for that I am happy."

"Happy enough to throw a party?"

"Ya damn skippy. What better way to begin again? Hell, I need it, because from the snippets of convo I overhear from the kids, Kenny and Isis are hot and heavy."

"Benét, you know how sorry I am about your marriage, don't you? Yeah, you messed up, but I believed in the love the two of you had together so much that I thought it could withstand any blow."

"Yeah, I did too," Benét said on a sniffle. "But I am learning to deal with it. It isn't easy, seeing the man you love happy with someone other than you, but such is life. I can't dwell on that, Shaeyla, or I will go crazy."

"Well then we're going to throw one helluva party. I'll set Bilal on scoping out a spot. We'll do this one big."

Shaeyla heard Benét's doorbell chime in the background. "Hmmm, company huh?"

"Yes, and before you say anything it's Christian."

"Hey, I'm not saying a word. You do what makes you happy."

"Thanks. Call me tomorrow and let me know how things went."

As Shaeyla replaced the receiver she stretched her arms above her head and let out a squeal of delight. She could honestly say for the first time in a long time confident with herself and not afraid to speak her mind. It felt great.

S haeyla arrived at Jackson-Steele at nine sharp. She was anxious, but determined to have this conversation with both of the partners of Jackson-Steele.

Mitchell's assistant, Ms. Croghan, smiled as she approached the desk. "Good Morning, Ms. Andrews."

"Good morning."

"They asked that I send you in when you arrived. I've placed a coffee service and a tray of pastries in the conference room?"

"Thank you," I said as I walked to the conference room door. I knocked once before entering. Both men were standing near the window talking. Their conversation stopped when they saw me. Solomon was the first to break the silence.

"Good morning, Shaeyla," he said, helping me into my chair.

Mitchell just stood with one hand in his pocket as his eyes roamed over me.

"Good morning gentlemen," I said as I settled in my chair. They noticed that I made no move toward my briefcase. "I'm sure you're both wondering what this meeting is about?"

"The thought had crossed my mind," Mitchell stated as he took his seat beside Solomon.

"I want to talk about our relationship. Our private relationships," I said pointedly.

"Before you start, I think you should know-"

I cut Solomon off mid-sentence. "No, you must know that I was surprised to find out about your past the way that I did. But I can see that you're in love with Vanessa. I wish you the best of luck." I smiled to show him that there were no hard feelings.

He turned to Mitchell and extended his hand, "She's wanted you all along, take care of her."

Mitchell grasped his hand. "The best man won." His arrogance was too much for her.

"No Mitchell, the best man lost."

He gave her a look of perplexity.

"The best man lost. I came here to tell you both that I am removing myself from both of your lives. I want a man that wants me. More importantly, I want a man that *can* spend time with me. A man that will cherish me, love me, desire me, and is passionate for me. He will support my company, be my companion, my lover, and my friend. The two of you were always preoccupied."

She turned to Mitchell; "You've always been preoccupied with your work and your daughter."

Turning to Solomon, "And now I can see that you were preoccupied with thoughts of Vanessa."

They both went to protest.

She held up her hand, staying their words. "No. There's no need to deny what I am saying. I know and more notably; *I see* the truth. We all must move on. Our season of being with each other is at an end. I know that I was trying to make a relationship that wasn't going to work, work."

That statement she directed at Mitchell. "As much as I tried, deep in my heart, I knew we could never work. You never respected me from the beginning, so why would you respect me now? I know you. It was a game for you to come after me, because you cannot stand to lose. Deep in my heart, I always knew that you would never give me the relationship that I wanted. When in reality, we've lost the most precious thing of all -- time."

I reached inside my briefcase and retrieved two manila folders, handing one to each of them. "Having said that, I hope this won't put a strain on our business relationship. However, should this pose a problem, I have prepared a list of companies whose services are on par with mine."

They looked through the packet and noticed the papers she had drawn up in the event their talk went south.

"We are contracted for two more events. At the conclusion of the final event, our contract ends. I hope that Jackson-Steele will renew."

Mitchell and Solomon looked at each other before turning their eyes to her.

Solomon spoke for them both. "I always knew you were a class act, and today proved it. This is business and I am confident that we can work together now and in the future."

He got up from his chair and walked to her, pulling her to her feet. He kissed her on the cheek, "Any man will be lucky to have a jewel like you. Don't sell yourself short, because you deserve the best."

He retrieved his folder and turned to walk out the door leaving her alone with Mitchell.

She began to gather up her belongings.

Mitchell walked around the table to stand beside her.

"Solomon is right. You were unlike any other woman I had dealt with, yet I treated you exactly like them. For that I apologize." She heard the humbleness in his voice. Good he needed to be humbled. Having his ego dropped and his arrogance kicked.

She smiled, and turned to walk out the room.

"Take care," she threw over her shoulder as she exited through the door.

She felt great. Her business is intact and *finally* her life is her own. As she drove home she vowed to herself to concentrate on herself and her business. She was going to give men a break—for now. She needed to revisit Shaeyla and find out exactly what it was she wanted, needed, and desired to have in her life. What would truly fulfill her and make her happy? As she marinated on the question an idea popped into her head.

As she parked the car in her garage, she said aloud "Time for a girl's night out party."

Swiftly moving from her car, she raced into her house. Moving through the kitchen to her office, she sat at her desk, pulled out a pen and began her plans.

Kendall sat across from Isis, wondering what in the hell he was doing there. He eyed the beautiful brown beauty and found her wanting in so many areas. He might as well face facts, he loves his wife, he wants his wife, and it is time for him to fight for his wife.

"Kenny, are you listening to me?" Isis asked. Her voice was irritated. She had been talking about the forthcoming weekend.

"I'm sorry. What were you saying?" Kenny asked distractedly.

"What's wrong?" Isis asked, "You haven't heard a word I said all evening."

Kenny wiped his hands down his legs then placed them on top of the table. His hands were clasped tightly because of what he had to say. "Isis, listen. You're a fantastic woman, but I have to be honest with you. I am still very much in love with my wife."

Isis sat back in shock. She had truly believed in her mind that they were growing closer. They shared so much interest and spent most of their time together. But she had to face it, she always felt like his attention was elsewhere. *Like he was always distracted.*

Kendall watched the play of emotions cross over Isis' face. He reached across the table for her hand, "I am very

sorry to have led you to believe that we could ever be anything other than friends."

Isis kept her eyes on their clasped hands, "Its okay. I'd
rather you tell me now instead of later. But I have to ask
you a question."

"Yes."

"Are you sure you know what you're doing? I mean
does your wife feel the same way about you?"

Kendall sat back in his seat and released his hands
from hers. His heart was pounding. He wondered if he
had ruined his chances with Benét. The last time they
spoke he was still upset and was not very cordial to her.

"I don't know. But I am going to do everything in my
power to change her mind."

Isis stood up and grabbed her purse from the chair.
She walked around the table and leaned down to give
Kendall a parting kiss on his cheek.

"Take care," she said as she turned and walked away.

Kendall sat there for few minutes before going into action. He threw some bills down on the table and headed
to the door. He jogged across the lot to his truck, opened
the door and headed in the direction of Benét's.

• • • • •

Benét and Christian were watching a movie when her
doorbell rang. Christian looked at her with a question in
his eyes.

"What? I have no idea who that could be," she threw
over her shoulder as she made her way to her front door.

"Who is it?" she called as she approached the door.

No one answered. She could see a silhouette of the person through the frosted double glass doors. Moving to the side window she peered out into the dark and noticed Kendall's truck in the driveway.

Her eyes darted from side to side nervously. *What was he doing here?* She asked herself.

"Who is it?" Christian yelled from the living room.

"Benét, its Kendall. Please, open the door, I have to talk to you?"

Gathering her wits about her, she straightened and moved to the door. Nervously, she swept her hair behind her ear and opened the door. He stood there and for seconds said nothing at all.

They stared at each other, drinking in the sight of each other.

Kendall cleared his throat, "Can I come in?"

Benét looked over her shoulder, "Well right now is not a good time Kenny," she said continuing to look over her shoulder, concerned that at any moment Christian would appear.

"Oh, so Kane is here?"

"Yes."

Kendall stepped over the threshold. "Benét, we really need to talk."

"About what, Kenny?"

"About us."

"What about us? I thought you said what you had to say when we met a while back."

Kendall looked at his wife and knew he had to tell her

he loved her. He stepped forward again and took her face in his hands.

"Benét, I love you."

Benét's heartbeat tripled. It was beating so hard she thought he could hear it. "Kendall…" She didn't know what to say.

"I love you, Benét."

Benét was speechless. "Why now?"

Kendall was about to answer when he saw Christian entering the room.

Benét watched Kendall's eyes focus on a spot behind her. She knew that Christian had walked into the room.

"Benét, is everything okay?" Christian asked as he walked up behind her and placed a proprietal hand around her waist.

Kendall went rigid with anger when he saw the hand that Christian placed on Benét's waist.

"Stay out of this Kane!" Kendall blurted.

Christian lurched around Benét towards Kendall. He placed a finger in his face.

"Whatever happens to Benét *is* my business!" Christian said with a measured control Benét had never seen him portray.

Stepping between the two gentlemen she turned to Christian. "Please. I need to talk Kendall alone."

Christian was crestfallen. "Benét-."

"Please Christian. I need to hear what he has to say."

Christian's eyes bored into Benét as if he found the answers he was looking for. His heart was racing. He needed her assurance either orally or silently that she still loved him. That she still wanted him. Instead he saw confusion and a glint of hope.

Kendall watched the nonverbal communication between the two of them and knew he had to do what he must to put his marriage on the right track.

Benét crossed the foyer to Kendall's study. Out of all the changes she'd made to her home, the study still bore Kendall's mark. She still thought of it as *his* room.

Kendall was taken aback as he stepped into the room. It was obvious that Benét had left the room as it was. As if she was waiting for him to come home. The kids had told him how she had made subtle changes to the main rooms of the house, which he noted on his entry. But his study was just that, *his*. From the paperweight on his desk blotter to the books on the shelves, the entire room was Kendall's; even the photo of the two of them on their first year anniversary sat on his desk.

Crossing over to the photo he picked it up and turned it to Benét. "I was so happy when we took this." Kendall placed the photo back in its place. "You know what I thought when we took that?"

Benét shook her head negatively.

Kendall raised his head, "I thought about how much I loved you and how I never wanted to lose you."

Benét moved forward. These are the words she's been waiting months to hear from her husband. Her last attempt to get him to resolve their issues and give their marriage a try had been for naught. So in her mind she'd move on with Christian. Three months ago, she would've jumped to be back with him. Now, she wasn't sure.

Kendall watched the uncertainty cross Benét's face. He knew how stubborn she could be.

"Kendall, three months ago when we met at Carembe..." she started.

Kendall cut her off. "Three months ago, I was still in pain. I was still feeling betrayed, and wronged by you."

Benét was shaking her head; "I want to believe you so much right now Kendall..."

Kendall reached out and took her hands in his, "I need you to believe that I am so sorry for driving you away from me. But at the time, every time I looked at you, I saw you with *him*. Images of the two of you played like a recorder in my mind constantly rewinding back to a scene of the two of you making love."

Benét felt him shudder as he spoke. She placed her hand on his cheek. "I do love you, Kendall. It's just that right now -- right now, I need time to think."

Kendall stiffened in her arms. He didn't remark, he just pulled her body closer to his. She felt so good in his arms. He inhaled deeply of *that scent* that was special to him. She smelled like she always did soft, delicate, and light.

Benét pulled away from him. Christian was in the other room and she had to get away from both men to clear her head. She moved to the door and stepped back into the foyer.

Kendall knew that was his cue to leave. Without a

word he walked past her, but as he reached the entry door he turned, "I'm going to do whatever it is I have to do to change your mind."

As the door closed Christian asked, "Change your mind about what?"

Benét froze. She hated being questioned. She didn't answer his question.

"Christian, we have to talk, but before we do that I have some serious thinking that I have to do. Alone. See yourself out, please."

She didn't say anymore. She strode past him to the steps to take her to her bedroom.

Chapter 48 - The After Party

S haeyla watched the fireworks from her harbor view room. Once again she was alone, but this time it wasn't the end of the world like she used to think. This year she had resolved to put herself first and she did that. She understands that she is worthy of love, trust, and commitment from that special someone. She had pinned her hopes on two very dynamic and different men and neither turned out to be the loves of her life. She realized now that she had built Mitchell and Solomon up in her own mind to be more than what they were. They are both equally good men, yet they were not good for *her*. A year ago, more than anything admitting this would have hurt her. She would have believed that the end of both of the relationships was her fault, but she has grown and matured emotionally over the past year. She has watched death take a toll on Kendra and Niall's fragile relationship, yet they persevered. She saw Benét humbled over her own selfish actions and witnessed vulnerability she hadn't seen her girl show in over twenty years. What started out as a blessed event for Diandra and Seven, turned into a tragedy of Diandra's own selfish & reckless behavior. Finally, she watched Worthy in her tumultuous struggle against addiction. Shaeyla counted her blessings and reveled in the thoughts of the love she had for her friends.

Another year of drama, pain, and glory, only strength-ened our bond, which proves that our friendship can with-stand all bumps, hills, and hurdles in our path. She held up her glass to herself and toasted to her health and happiness. As she sipped on the expensive bubbly, a genuine smiled crossed her face. *This is the first time I didn't throw a party!*